Mistress of the Golden Cords

The Fifth Tale from the Dragonsbane Inn

By

Adam Berk

Mistress of the Golden Cords

The Fifth Tale from the Dragonsbane Inn

Adam Berk

Cover Art by Jeff Ward

Copyright © 2019 Adam Berk

All rights reserved.

This book is a work of fiction. Names, characters, places and incidents are either a product of the author's imagination or used fictionally. Any resemblance to actual events, locals, or persons living or dead is either satiric or entirely coincidental.

ISBN: **9781698371870**

To my original editor, hype man, and bar brother Damon Farese. You've set my standards: if I can get you to pause Final Fantasy and Zelda long enough to read these, I'll know I've done my job.

Books by Adam Berk

The Centaur & the Sot

The Trouble with Trolls

The Swap

On the Wings of Draklings

Mistres of the Golden Cords

Charms (forthcoming)

Adam Berk

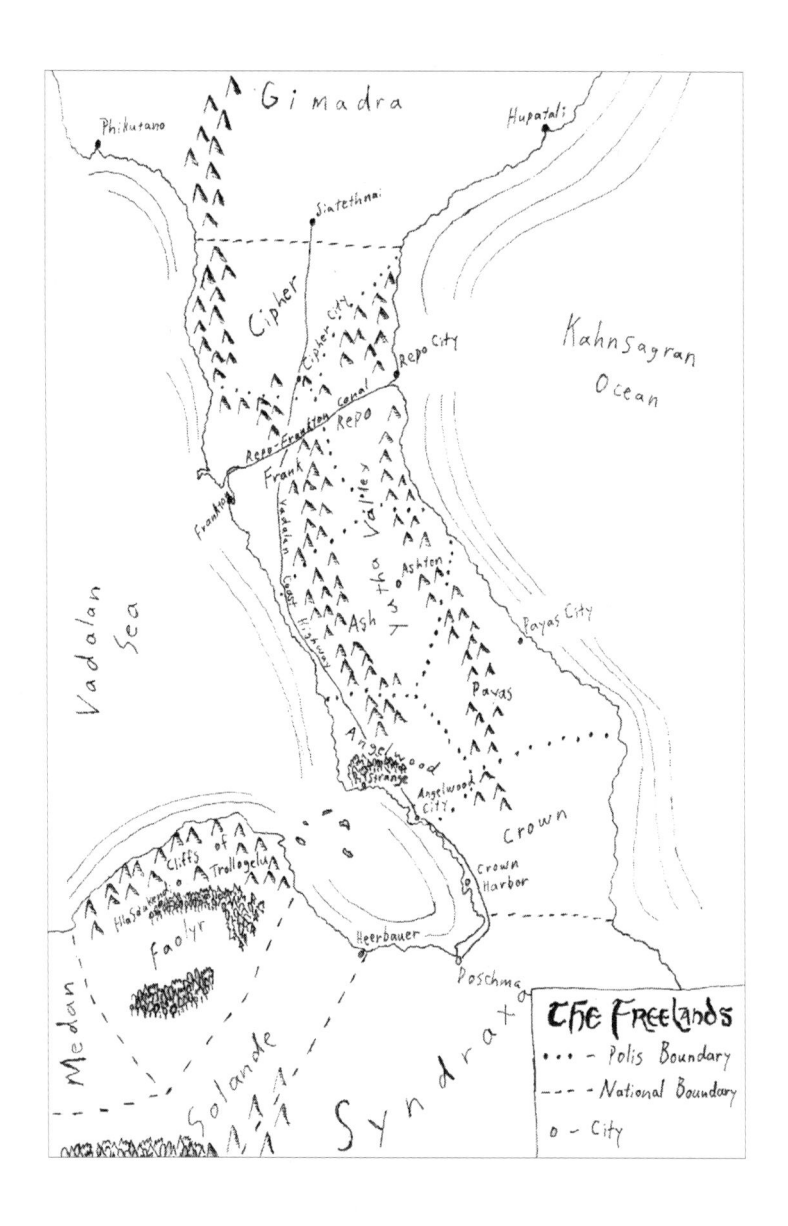

Note: Resemblance between The Freelands of Ardyn and other fantasy lands may not be entirely coincidental

~ I ~

Anticipation buzzed about the dressmaker's tent in swarms of giggles. The Siren, Kitana, was due to perform at The Pit – the most renowned amphitheater in all the Freelands – and Maggie was killing time before curtain with her friend Trina at one of the many vendors surrounding the venue. But to see the younger barmaid frolic amongst the Syndraxan silk, Gimadran featherflax, and Alsyran wool, you'd have thought the modest boutique itself was the evening's main event.

"How 'bout this one?"

Maggie wrinkled her nose. "Feh! If I'm gonna pay that much for a fancy dress, it ought'ta look more interesting than that!"

"Ah, go'n, Mags," Trina pouted playfully as she twirled, the fine silk gown shimmering emerald green as she held it over her humble brown skirts. "The color's perfect for you. I know the cut's a bit guvny, but teats like yours could turn an Devandracal nun's robe into a satyr's sex cloak!"

A startled guffaw burst from Maggie's voluptuous frame. Flobbing about with her young co-worker often seemed like having two friends in the same body. One moment the fair, fine-boned barmaid would be all innocence and poise, the next she'd tell a joke so lewd it'd send even the worldly wenches at

Mistress of the Golden Cords

the Dragonsbane Inn into fits of tittering. Such were Trina's bawdy humor and free spirit that Maggie couldn't help but love her, despite her gods-awful perfect looks.

Until now, the older barmaid had never done well with attractive girlfriends. This was Angelwood after all, where the pretty girls danced and sang, flaunting their lithe young bodies with as little care and as few thoughts as possible. Maggie'd lived here all her life, and had lost count of all the times her unmanageable red hair and plump physique led to packs of vacky, dim-witted vixes treating her as though she had a debilitating illness. Fortunately, the snickering and sneers had lost their sting over the years, and the barmaid hadn't cried over any of that shest since grade school.

Well, not publicly, at least.

"Oh!" Trina exclaimed. "How about this one for me! Isn't this just the most perfect shade of blue you've ever seen?"

"Why not try it on?" Maggie laughed. "I've already seen you in everything else in the shop!"

"I love looking good, okay? It's like Sean de Siurteen said, 'Beauty is the handwriting of the gods.'"

"Who?"

"Tyrnish philosopher. Wrote 'Nature and the Mirror' in 1378 about the artist's place in society?"

Maggie peered at the girl as though she could catch a glimpse of whatever mischievous sprite was pulling cranks and levers inside the barmaid's head at random.

"Trina, no offense, but you are the strangest person I've ever worked with."

"None taken. Genius is just madness with applause, I always say."

"Ever thought of going to Angelwood University? You clearly got more smarts than ya know what to do with."

"Oh, I'd love to! Then I'll buy my own ship and go sailing to the Greatlands! Have you any idea what that pocking school charges for admission?"

"Don't be so quick to pish it off. I know wenches who've scraped enough together for a basic degree. What would you study if you *could* go?"

"Antiquities," she said, not even stopping to consider. "I've always loved reading about the ruins of Empyrrica or the old Alsyranian and Medanian Empires. Plus, antiquarians get to travel!"

Maggie thought of Trina with her coifed golden hair and pretty dresses dredging for artifacts in some peat bog in the Northern Wastes and laughed loudly.

"Sorry, dolly," she said to the girl's puzzled frown. "It's just that you'd be the best dressed digger at the site, that's for certain!"

Trina blushed and lowered her eyes with a small smile.

"I just like looking pretty, that's all."

Suddenly, outside the dressmaker's tent, the clamor of the milling crowds softened to an excited murmur. The barmaids cocked their heads, listening. For a moment, there was nothing but the eerie silence spreading throughout the busy marketplace. But then they heard the drums.

THU-thu-thu-thu-THUD!

They looked at each other. Trina grinned with delight, and Maggie laughed with elation. Before they knew it, they were rushing out the door of the tent, sandals thumping over the gleaming white planks of the Pride Walk: the vendor-lined boardwalk surrounding The Pit, the grandest amphitheater in all the Freelands!

They moved as though pulled on invisible strings. The ground shook with the thump of approaching drums. The air burst to life with the blare of trumpets and criers shouting for theatergoers to enter and find their seats before the show began.

They found their companions, the barkeeps Garret and Farian at an ale crafter's tent. Farian, of course, was chatting up the aleman's "barmaid", a long-legged blonde wares hawker with skirts too short and blouse too low-cut to be useful as real working attire. Garret, ever the practical master barkeep, talked shop with the brewer behind the counter, broad shoulders swaying, paunch jiggling with mirth, and bald head

Mistress of the Golden Cords

flushing as he sampled tumbler after tumbler of the merchant's products.

Trina bounded into the tent and threw her arms around Garret's neck. The big man returned her embrace, lifting her easily off her feet. If the girl was put off at all by the ale froth on the senior barkeep's bristly goatee, she gave no indication.

Maggie looked at the couple the same way she'd once stared at a gold fenmark tip left by a shabby goblin day laborer. Alien as Trina's tastes and tendencies might be to Angelwood's superficial norms, the sight of her and the barkeep together just didn't make sense. Maggie had known Garret for the past ten years when they'd begun working at the Dragonsbane together, and they'd grown into the closest of friends. He'd always been level-headed when it came to women, rolling his eyes at the aspiring dancers or performers that came to the bar, saying they were more interested in exhibitionistic nonsense than learning an honest trade.

True, Trina'd never expressed any interest in song, dance, or exhibitionism, but she *was* at an age where her own interests and identity were the meat and potatoes of her life, and her relationships with others only gravy. It was near the age Garret's daughter might be if he'd ever had one. The idea made Maggie cringe. Not so much with disgust, she told herself, but at the prospect of her old friend's battered heart weathering yet another crushing disappointment.

"Ho, everyone!" she said, interrupting her own reverie along with her companions' gratuitous canoodling. "Sun's almost down. We should head back to the entrance if we want to catch Kit before the show."

"Pock, yes!" Farian exclaimed. "Garret, hurry up and finish your ale! If you pish my chance to meet a real live *siren*, I'll go hedwig on ya kull!"

"All right, keep ya breeches up," said Garret as he exchanged three copper cujots for an enormous, frothy tankard of Berserker Brown. "Not like she'll be any different from any other woman without all those glamour spells and ether effects; certainly no more beautiful than this one 'ere."

Adam Berk

He caught Trina's delicate arm with his scarred bear claw of a hand and twirled her –quite gently for such a lumbering mountain troll of a man – into his arms.

"Dreffy, Love, very dreffy," she said, rolling her eyes as she smiled up at him. "But coming from you it's nice and sweet."

They kissed again, and Maggie averted her eyes in spite of herself.

Meanwhile, down the bar a ways, Farian took the opportunity to slip an arm around the blonde ware hawker's waist and whisper something in her ear that made her blush, gasp, and slap his face, although not as hard as she might have. He smiled, said something impudent and charming, and the girl blushed prettily. Looking over her shoulder, the apprentice barkeep shot Maggie the sliest of winks, with dark eyes as radiant as his fine doublet, a wolfish smile, and impeccable hair.

Always on the prowl, that one, Maggie thought. *But that's what comes o' hiring a minstrel as a barkeep. Not that there's much else to choose from in this polis.*

Garret had been turning the young man from an itinerant hustler into a respectable member of the Publican's Guild, but she wondered how much influence went the other way as well.

But, Maggie thought as she herded her friends out the door, now was not the time for personal drama. The barmaid had procured trap room access chops for the four of them to meet the renowned siren Kitana, whom Maggie had known back in grammar school as Kathryn Brunholme. So Garret downed his ale in a mighty gal-ulp, Farian made his final attempt to capture the ale seller's heart (or any other parts left unguarded), before they all four bounded over the boards to The Pit's backstage entrance.

A pair of stavemen, black leather armor gleaming in the light of the setting sun, guarded the door with quarterstaffs crossed at precisely the right point to block their progress. Maggie opened her purse and produced four white wooden chips with roaring lion's heads stamped on red wax. One of the guards took the tokens, inspected them closely, and gave

Mistress of the Golden Cords

his fellow a solemn nod before they pulled their staffs aside. The door behind them swung inward, pulled by an unseen mechanism, and the group entered, mouths and eyes agog with unabashed excitement.

An Angelwood native, Maggie had been to The Pit many times, but this was the first she'd entered through the performers door. In prior visits she'd been pushed along in a throng of spectators, through mighty marble archways depicting the arena's patron deities: the small yet sensuous goddess Demia, and the proud, straight-backed god Incubaal, his massive bare chest, framed by swirling regal robes. Murals on every wall depicted famous performers in violent and dramatic scenes, and famous weapons and props from plays hung on thin cords from the high, domed ceiling. In the midst of it all had stood a fabulous bronze statue of The Pit's founder, the great bard, Symonde Lyonscall, and below it the inscription: "For the glory of all arts".

Now, as the stavemen escorted her and her friends through the arena's lantern-lit backstage corridors, Maggie saw that the performers entrance had an impressiveness all its own. Squires and assistants scurried every which way with costumes and props, fiddled with complex apparatuses with curved mirrors and glowing crystals, and swung on ropes and ladders careening in every direction. Through it all, the lead staveman rattled off a well-rehearsed soliloquy about the importance of keeping to designated zones at all times, how each performance's magical enhancements required flawless precision, and how a single distracted stagehand could destroy the entire performance. All was said with stiff-jawed solemnity, but Maggie, noting the excited gleam in the security officer's eyes, could tell that this too was part of the act.

"Why, Maggie UiCrielvan! It is *so* good to see you, dolly! How long's it been?"

Kit rushed to greet them as soon as they entered her trap room – the room in which a performer dons her or his trappings and makeup before the performance.

How long? thought Maggie as the siren threw her slender

arms around her neck in a warm embrace. *Well, Kit, if you mean how long since we last talked, it was last Eccoday when I served you at the inn, and you gave me the access chops. Since we were in school together? That would be fifteen years. Since we flobbed about as friends? Never.*

Maggie introduced Kit to her friends and she hugged each of them in turn. The barmaid had to admit one thing about the siren: she was spectacular! Her eyes were large and dazzling as emeralds, her lustrous, raven hair fell perfectly about her delicate shoulders with every fluid movement she made. Likewise, her costume, little more than draped streamers of green silk and purple gauze, slid every which way across her smooth, toned flesh, always revealing just enough to seduce without shocking – much!

Kitana flitted through the room, introducing the party to her retinue of representatives and assistants, inviting them to sit upon any of the room's assorted ottomans, couches, and chaise lounges and to enjoy any of the various platters of sweets and charcuteries scattered throughout. Being barkeeps, Farian and Garret were conditioned to pounce on free food like starving manticores whenever offered and fell upon the victuals with gusto.

Maggie, meanwhile, admired the balance of aesthetics and functionality of the room itself. There were racks of fine clothes arranged by color (mostly black and different shades of green), colorful draperies on the walls, matching floral arrangements in every corner, and mirrors so Kit might see herself reflected at any angle.

The barmaid also noted, to her amusement, those parts of the room not quite covered by flowers and frills. The only thing that drew greater crowds to The Pit than siren shows were the duels, melees, and mock battles performed by the arena's staff of professional fighters, and signs of their presence peeked around every corner. There were solid wooden racks and hooks embedded in the sandstone walls for hanging weapons, a leather-padded surgeon's table, and a terra cotta tiled bathing area in a corner for the gladiatorial combatants to wash off the blood, sweat, and sand of the

Mistress of the Golden Cords

arena. For all its splendor, Kit's trap room was no more than a clever arrangement of fripperies, to be flipped and refurnished for whatever player or performer next needed its services.

An old Freelandish joke about Pit performers never defecating in the same place twice popped into Maggie's mind, and she turned to Trina to share it. The girl turned out to be cornered, however, by two of Kitana's representatives – her venue facilitator, a portly goblin named Tauni Miskmunn, and her talent emissary, a trow elf whom she'd introduced simply as "Nige". Both were dressed in the height of fashion, Nige in a frilled black and gold doublet, Tauni in emerald, silk robes fashioned after those of the Lascivian Mages. Both fawned over the young barmaid with smiles wolves might wear while asking a plump little rabbit to be the guest of honor at their dinner party.

"No," she told them, "I don't have any representation. Nor any *talent*, for that matter, which rather makes the issue moot, doesn't it?"

"Not as much as you'd think," said Tauni, his wide, friendly grin undermined by his beady yellow eyes and tusks protruding from a prominent underbite. "Talent can be taught, bought, or entirely forgot so long as you're selling tickets at peak prices: gettin' the kulls in the seats, like we say."

"What my dear friend Tauni means," Nige chimed in. He was a bit taller than Tauni, with fine, chiseled features that would have been attractive were he not wearing an obvious layer of faux-bronze makeup. "Is that when it comes to deciding which performers to represent, men in our professions need only ask three questions: when the performer walks through the marketplace and all eyes are on her, how many want to pock her, how many want to kill her, and how many want to *be* her?"

As though she were a cut of meat at the butcher's, Maggie thought.

She nearly interjected on her friend's behalf, but held back when she saw the younger barmaid's expression. She was listening with a shrewd half-smile, not the goggle-eyed golly-face most Freelandish girls got when they talked to entertainment professionals. Maggie decided she wanted to see how the girl handled herself here, though whether from respect or rivalry she couldn't say.

"The higher the all around numbers," the elvish emissary continued, "the more successful the siren. And the numbers for each question in particular—"

"Determines the *type* of siren she's to be," said Trina, "and how you sell her to the public. I'm familiar with the concept. My uncle's the impresario for a troupe of players."

"Oh? Which troupe, if you don't mind me asking?"

"The Sylvan Guild."

The elf's eyes bulged and the goblin nearly fell over in surprise.

Oh boy! Here we go. Blood in the water.

"The *Sylvan Guild!*" Miskmunn sputtered. "*The* Sylvan Guild! That's Shossy UiConnall's troupe. Nige! We're talkin' to Shossy UiConnall's *niece* here!"

"Yes, Tauni; I deduced as much myself. Well, young lady, it seems we've misjudged you. Clearly if you had interests in the performing arts, you'd be well equipped to pursue them. I mean, most girls with such a renowned impresario for an uncle would be well on their way to sirendom by now."

"No, it's not that," said Trina, her voice going soft. "Uncle Shosev and me, we had a sort of – disagreement. We haven't spoken in two years."

"Ah! Of course," said Nige, with a grandly dismissive long-fingered wave. "Say no more. Family! It's no accident the most famous plays are about feuding relatives.

"Listen, I have offices at the old Steward Brothers Playhouse. You know where that is, right? Creeper Street between Aurora Boulevard and Wellspring Way? I'm holding auditions for new talent next Arbiday if you'd care to stop by."

"Oh, I don't know about that. Besides, I think I'm working that day."

"The barmaid job? Oh, I'm sure you can get that covered sometime in the next eight days. Unless you think bringing

Mistress of the Golden Cords

people food and drink is a better use of your time than testing your chops on stage."

"No, no. It sounds thrilling, it's just—"

"You don't think a life of magic, wealth, and fame would hold your interest as well as the fascinating world of a serving wench?"

"The whole thing sounds very, um, interesting. It's just—"

"Oh, it's interesting, all right." Maggie interjected. She didn't know what had put the muzzle on Trina's biting wit, but seeing her friend getting cozened by these two hustlers brought out the mama bear in her.

"Bit like studying the mating habits of tine worms, innit?" she continued. "Trina, I'll bet if you fenmarks to fish fins they wouldn't be anywhere near this persistent if you hadn't mentioned your famous uncle."

"Oh, ho! Tine worms, she says," Tauni hissed, porcine nostrils flaring, pointy ears twitching, and a sweaty sheen rising to his greenish complexion. "As though we're all just bloodsucking parasites, eh, Nige? How droll! And she clearly knows *so* much about show business!"

"Your words, dolly."

"Now, now," Nige purred, running delicate fingers through his long, dark hair, "there's no need for personal invectives. It so happens that Tauni and I noticed a certain potential in the young lady."

"And by potential, I'm sure you mean a winning combination of perky teats and insecurity. Maybe you could trick her into signing a contract where all moneys from performances go to 'production expenses' while she's paid a pittance like the siren Cassandra Clerksyn. Or maybe you could get her hooked on amphite crystals like Whisteria the White. Or have your rich buddies pay to gang rape her like Licentia of the Lilacs."

"That was never proven!"

Tauni sputtered in outrage, while Nige stared in openmouthed awe at Maggie's bilious bluntness. Before their altercation could escalate further, however, Kitana appeared, inserting herself with surgical precision.

"Gentlemen, gentlemen," she said with a smile that could melt marble, "I am so sorry, but I neglected to mention that my dearest Maggie-wags has lived in Angelwood *all* her life and will immediately smell any trollshest you mean to foist upon her. No, don't debate me on this. I won't hear it. It's all trollshest, every bit of it, and you two are holding the biggest shovels. So run along now and do the jobs I give you a quarter of my moneys to perform while I entertain my guests."

The siren waved them away. They bowed, oozing with superficial acquiescence and wearing the same unnatural smile, then bustled off gesticulating to one another in low, urgent tones. Maggie didn't presume to know what they discussed, but she did catch the phrases "waste of potential", "always keep our crystals in-case", and "still take tea with ol' Shossy some time. Maybe next Compraday !"

"I do apologize for my assistants' behavior," said the siren, touching Maggie's shoulder and fondling a lock of her hair as though it were exquisite jewelry. "There's never a moment when those two aren't scouting and hustling, and your friend clearly has potential."

"Ah, g'on, Kit," said Maggie, blushing a little. "It's me that should apologize. I just remember how exploited *you* were in your early days, and it got my mama hen's feathers ruffled, that's all."

"Quite all right, dollykins, quite all right. Truth to tell, I could *use* a little mothering these days."

Kitana gave her a hug and a kiss on both cheeks, just as she always did the handful of times they'd run into each other over the years. As she did, Maggie was appalled, though not surprised, at how many of the girl's ribs she could feel beneath her dress. Likewise, she noted the sunken eyes and meaty stench in her breath coming from too many hours spent rehearsing, performing, and appearing at social engagements, and not enough on proper nutrition and rest. In contrast, strangely enough, her breasts and buttocks appeared to be not only firm and healthier than the rest of her, but larger than the

Mistress of the Golden Cords

barmaid remembered.

"Um, excuse me," said Trina with an incredulous giggle, "but am I missing something here? I don't sing. I don't dance. Just what sort of *potential* are we talking about?"

"Difficult to say, my dove," said Kitana turning with a casually splendid swirl of silk and raven tresses, and looking the girl over from top to bottom. "The priestesses at the Temple of the Cavorting Incarnate describe it as a sort of *openness*. As if you're a perfect vessel to receive the presence of the Goddess Demia."

"The Temple of the—?"

"Cavorting Incarnate. It refers to the divine dance through which Demia the Unbound gained mastery over the great god Incubaal by binding him with golden cords. I have some literature here somewhere."

The siren twirled about and glided to a nearby vanity, where she began to poke through its delicate array of tiny drawers.

Ah, here we go again, thought Maggie. *Pocking Angelwood and its entertainment trades. If they can't snare your heart or your head, they'll capture your soul instead!*

"Kit," said the barmaid, "don't let us keep you. I know your show starts in less than an hour, if you'd rather save this for afterward."

"Oh, nonsense, Maggie," Kitana replied between jumbles of perfume bottles and tangled jewelry. "You know I can never keep a thought in my head for more than a moment after a show. If it's not here then – ah-ha!"

She turned about, holding up a pamphlet triumphantly. Its title, *Desire's Dance: Mastering the Art of Wantcraft*, stood on its cover in a grandly embellished hand. The letters had the telltale bluish shimmer of replicating parchment. Trina took the piece in both hands as though she thought it might sprout wings and fly away.

Maggie's respect for the girl plummeted.

Oh come now, Trina. Tell me you're not that much of a dim dolly! You told me you've lived in Angelwood seven years. In all that time no one's *warned you about the Demian cult?*

"Desire," said Trina. "Does that mean my desire or the desires of others?"

"Both," said Kit, "and more. When you take a lover is it because you want it, or because he wants it? Or is it something else entirely? Something that's bigger than both of you?"

Trina stood in silence. It seemed as though she wanted to ask a question, but was unsure what that question could be.

Arda! What am I going to do with this girl? How can she be so clever and so naïve at the same time?

Maggie was about to give Trina her two cujots worth, but right then a stagehand rushed to the siren and told her she had a quarter cup until show time. They made their goodbyes, and the stavemen returned to escort them to their seats. Garret and Farian nudged and clapped each other on the backs over the things they'd do to Kitana and any number of other sirens if only they were rich and famous enough. Trina flipped through the pamphlet casually at first, then with growing interest.

"This says desire is one of the great magical forces of the world," she prattled. "Like fire or running water or drymist in etherhouses. And if someone learns how to master that force, they can accomplish anything. And it makes sense, you know? Like what Kitana said about desire being greater than two people who feel it. I know sometimes when I'm with Garret—"

"Listen," Maggie snapped in a low voice. She'd heard this tune many times before and, after thirty-five years living in this depraved polis, its melody made her want to vomit. "I didn't want to say anything in front of Kit, but you should know that the Demian temple isn't all it's vaunted to be."

"What do you mean?"

"Well, Kit swears by their teachings, and they've done just fine by her career-wise. But she's not the same person she was when she joined. It's as though she dun't have no real joy in anything anymore."

"She seemed happy to me."

Mistress of the Golden Cords

"Of course she did. But that's her job, innit? Smile and charm, day in and day out. Meanwhile, she han't seen friends, family, or a real relationship in years."

"With some families that might not be so bad," Trina said with a scowl.

Maggie sighed, remembering when she heard about Trina's "disagreement" with her Uncle Shosev. Four moons ago, a week before Sunderfest, they'd been closing the Dragonsbane's common room, putting up benches and pulling soiled floor reeds, when the elder barmaid had asked the girl if she'd made any plans for the coming holiday. Trina had said she had not, which had led to Maggie inquiring about her family.

Now Maggie had not meant to pry, but she did have an insatiable curiosity when it came to the private affairs of others. Being privy to such things was one of the few great joys of a barmaid's life, after all. But even the senior barmaid was taken aback when an innocuous question about her one local family member sent the younger wench into a fit of red-faced, snot-bubbling sobs. It took a while for the girl to get a hold of herself, and when she finally had, told a sordid tale.

She'd first come to Angelwood when she was thirteen, fleeing an arranged marriage by her parents back in Alsyra, and seeking sanctuary at the estate of her Uncle Shosev. Her uncle, so supportive and caring at first, turned out to be the worst kind of lecherous kullbung, attempting to coerce her into all manner of incestuous perversions, using her desperate situation as leverage. Finally she'd made her escape, striking him across the face with a bed warmer one night when his advances grew too bold. She'd fled to a friend's house with naught but her night shift and a purse with a dozen copper cutmarks. Maggie, after a moment's shock, had crushed the poor girl in a big-bosomed hug, insisted she spend Sunderfest with her and her family, and kept close to her in the weeks that followed.

"Anyway," Trina continued, voice rising despite sideward glances from nearby stagehands, "Kitana's *had* relationships! I heard she was sweet on some Pit fighter, Pyrick 'the Human

Spider' Gardener. Or was it Seamus Howlett the Berserker?"

"Both," Maggie replied, "and neither. She had a dalliance with the Human Spider after a party once, and she makes public appearances with the Berserker for publicity, but all the rest are rumors passed about by her assistants. Truth is, with her performance schedule, she han't got the time for eating or sleeping, let alone proper courtship."

The hardwood planks beneath their feet gave way to crunching sandy grist, and the group traded glances and grins as

they realized they were *on* the floor of the arena. In a few swift paces, they were lead to their seats, which were on a deck, painted black so as to be nearly invisible in the flickering light of oil lamps, enclosed by a simple rail, a mere stone's throw away from the stage where Kitana would be performing. They settled in, Trina and Garret sitting together, Farian and Maggie on either side.

"Oh, Mags," the younger barmaid was saying, "with Kitana's renown, I'm sure she could make time to have a personal life if she wanted one. And anyway, I don't think I'd have to be a wealthy, successful siren to benefit from the Demian temple's teachings."

"That's what I'm trying to tell you" Maggie groaned. "Those 'teachings' of theirs are the problem in the first place. Ho, Farian!"

She leaned over Trina, and the apprentice barkeep's head poked out from behind Garret's great bulk in response.

"You've been minstreling at the Demian temple, haven't you?" She had to yell to be heard above the babbling crowd.

"Every second Compraday," he yelled back.

"And what, pray tell, does that work entail?"

"Soft ballads and sonnets mostly. I play them in the garden. Helps create a certain ambience for the temple's visitors, if you know what I mean."

"Oh yeah. I get you teedee koke. Our young friend Trina here, however, does not. Enlighten her, if you please!"

"Ah-ha," said the part-time bard shaking his head with a

Mistress of the Golden Cords

chuckle. Then turning to the younger barmaid he said, "I'm not supposed to divulge any specific rites, but I can give you the gist of it in two words. Sanctified. Prostitution."

Trina's jaw dropped as she sat back in her seat with a "hmmf". She might have said more, but the lamps dimmed, trumpets and drums blared to life, and the show began, sweeping them and hundreds of others up in a spectacular rush of sex and sound.

~ II ~

Truly amazing, thought Trina, *how life can take you to the highest heights, then drop you straight into the nearest shest pile.*

She crumpled the note from her landlord and hurled it into her hearth.

Fourteen fenmarks! I moved in six months ago and he's raising my rent to fourteen pocking fenmarks a month. That's almost two week's wages!

She almost lit the hearth fire, just to watch the accursed parchment burn, but stopped herself. Wood and oil cost money, and there was still an hour of natural daylight to take advantage of before she began cooking dinner.

She crossed the room to the corner by the window where she sat most nights reading her beloved books. She stood a moment, waiting for the whirlwind of anxiety and the gods-I'm-so-broke thoughts in her head to subside, while she rested a hand on the side of her bookcase. The case was by far the most expensive piece in the room. She still had to pay the merchant she'd bought it from three more times if she didn't want it to get repossessed, but the emotional well-being she felt from its presence was worth every cujot. Its desert oak wood was lighter than the Alsyran oak in her parents' library, but the

Mistress of the Golden Cords

feel of it was comforting just the same.

She pulled a volume of *The Adventures of Dunn Novan* from its shelf, sending as she did the Demian pamphlet Kitana had given her tumbling to the floor. She froze a moment before picking it up, staring at it the way she might a new menu item ordered by a finicky customer. She'd planned to read it as soon as she got home from The Pit last corpday, but they'd stayed out later than expected, and after that, a busy weekend at work had pushed the literature to the back of he mind.

Sanctified prostitution, she thought, flipping through the coarse pulp pages. *There must be more to it than that. Well, now's not the time for that, anyway.*

Resolving to give it a thorough examination on her next day off, Trina sat in her rickety old rocking chair by the window, and tossed the pamphlet onto the sill. She opened her book, *The Adventures of Dunn Novan*, and tried to lose herself in the exploits of the legendary Trophican explorer. Unfortunately, even the tales of braving sea serpents on the Capacian Ocean and trading with the cat people of Mraugh couldn't compete with the maelstrom of bills and debts tearing through her mind.

Soon enough the daylight faded, Trina lit her lamps and hearth and fixed her dinner. As she ate her simple bowl of naano cornmeal and sausages, she made a mental list of ways to reduce her expenses or make more money. Maggie insisted her tips would increase as her skills as a barmaid improved and she could take more tables, but she was skeptical. Try as she might, she just couldn't focus her mind the way the other wenches did to remember orders a dozen at a time. Whenever she tried, that old whirlwind of anxieties would return, leaving her breathless and flustered.

She could, she supposed, always move in with Garret. A warm glow spread through her at the thought. The man might have been made of Alsyran oak himself for all his solid dependability. When he was with her she felt more solid herself, as though the countless troubles life threw at her just bounced off.

So what if they did live together? Such an arrangement would be unheard of back in Alsyra, or most other "old world" nations of the Mystican Commonwealth. But here in the Freelands, where everyone spent their transient lives chasing their own dreams and schemes, unbetrothed cohabitation was becoming more and more prevalent. Could the solution to all her problems really be so simple? Could she really live every day with Garret in such happiness, stability and peace?

She finished her last bite of cornmeal and sausage with a sigh and brought her bowl to the washbasin. As she poured a measure of water on it and scrubbed, she realized the thought of moving out of her flat made her sad. As challenging as it was, this was the first time in her life she'd ever had a place of her own. Good as life with her burly barkeep would no doubt be, thinking of moving in together now seemed as though she were giving up on herself: that the chance to discover the person she truly was would be gone forever.

She loved her little flat. She loved her personal sanctuary with her books, her rickety rocking chair, and the view of her building's courtyard from the window.

She used to read in the courtyard until one of her neighbors spoiled it. He'd sat beside her and tried seduce her by asking if she tasted as good as she looked. Then he'd licked her face.

But aside from the odd lunatic, lecher, or criminal, life she preferred being on her own. She loved the thrilling though terrifying sensation of having her own life in her own hands to fashion however she pleased. As she washed her face, undressed, and climbed into bed, she felt secure in her decision to keep her independence.

Hours later, she bolted upright, gulping air in high frantic gasps.

She'd had the dream again. Bony hands gripped her wrists. A great weight pressed her down. There was a pounding sensation like a hammer in her guts destroying her from the inside out.

That's my good girl. A phantom voice, husky yet smooth

breathed in her ear. *That's my little cat. My sweet, sweet little cat—*

Crying out in anger and disgust, she flung off her wet sheets and leaped off her straw mattress as though it were the fires of the abyss. Before she knew what she was doing she'd run into the front room, and sat on the floor in front of her bookcase hugging her knees to her chest.

I'm not going to cry, she thought. *Godsdamn it, just this once, I'm* not *going to cry!*

But, of course, she did, the sobs shaking her body like a leaf in a storm.

Eventually, the torrent of emotion subsided as it always did, leaving her drained. Sighing, she rose to her feet, lit the oil lamp by the window, and sat in her rocker, planning for a long, sleepless night. Though the creaks and cracks soothed her as she moved back and forth, she knew from experience she wouldn't be able to close her eyes until well into the next day.

Which means I'll be groggy all through my shift tomorrow, make more mistakes, take less tables, and make less money. Which means more anxiety about my bills and more sleepless nights – gods, Trina, what a pathetic mess you are! Maybe I should move in with Garret tomorrow, before he realizes how useless I am!

Seeking something – anything! – to take her mind off her troubles, she snatched the booklet off the windowsill. She opened it, read the first two paragraphs, then stopped and reread them carefully. Throughout the young barmaid's life, she'd read a vast number of books – the result of parents treating her as a precious possession to be locked away from the world. She knew, as all great readers do, that sometimes books did more than educate or tell stories. Sometimes they spoke to you, as though the words were friendly spirits sharing their observations of your life.

"In most traditional societies," the booklet said, "sex is depicted as a masculine conquest. The man pursues, and through persuasion or seduction, overcomes the woman's defenses in an act of intrusion.

But a woman's sexuality is more complex and, when it finds its counterpart in the ether, much more powerful. We don't merely penetrate: we bind, we tame, we alter men's very perceptions of reality."

Trina read the booklet cover to cover that night, and then read it again. By the time she finished the sun had risen, but strangely, she didn't feel tired. On the contrary, she was filled with a fire that wouldn't subside, even when buffeted by the strongest of storms.

Mistress of the Golden Cords

- III -

"Last call!" Garret bellowed in a voice that made the rafters shake. He grasped the rope of the brass bell mounted to the post between the house ale and cider casks, and snapped the clapper in three sharp strikes. He then readied himself for the last big push of the night: cleaning his spoons, strainers, and mixing pint, and checking his mixes, herbs, and garnishes.

Another good shift, he marveled as he watched the barmaids and dappers scurry about the common room taking their patrons' final drink orders.

The past few weeks at the Dragonsbane Inn had been uncharacteristically pleasant. His co-workers had done their jobs with confidence and efficiency. The clientele had been wealthier and less prone to complaints and brawls with their fellow guests.

Perhaps Master Wallingtok is finally starting to invest in some decent training and publicity.

He glanced at Trina UiConnall, then glanced again. She seemed to dance from one table to another, dazzling her parties with bright smiles and unshakable grace.

Then again, maybe I'm just seeing a bit more sunbeams than shadows these days. By the gods, how did a crusty old failure like me get so pocking lucky?

Adam Berk

Nothing could bother him today. His job seemed easy as breathing as servers flocked to the service well where the order slates began to pile up with the crisp clack-clacking that so often haunted his anxious dreams. His hands poured and mixed with speed and precision, but his mind kept wandering back to walks at sunset and candlelit suppers. To shared jokes and sweet sentiments told in soft voices under covers. To golden hair, and sparkling eyes, and skin so soft it make his great fumbling hands seem like stone by comparison.

"Garret, sweetie, that rumbullion cocktail's a crusta, not a swizzle."

Garret jerked away a bottle of lime juice, poured the drink back into a mixing tin and rimmed a glass with ground sugar cane before shaking, straining and garnishing with a honeypettle flower. He then spread the stack of remaining order slates in a row, and poured a shusheng hupatali, two beavertree sours, four glasses of brazenberry cider, and a brandywine punch before you could say "Slates in service!" Only then did he raise his gaze with a sheepish grin into the eyes of his beloved.

"And what're *you* thinking of that's got you so distracted?" she asked with a mischievous wink.

"That we both have the day off tomorrow," he replied, "and the rest of tonight if you don't mind staying a bit after closing."

"Well, aren't you the brazen one?" she teased. "The thought of it! Asking a girl out at this time of night. One might think you had jawdy designs on my virtue."

"Virtue? You? Your vices are more interesting if you ask me, dollita," he quipped smoothly, despite his reddening scalp.

Trina, arranging the drinks on her tray, tossed her head with mock indignation.

"Ha! What a rogue you are! And here I thought I had such a stable, responsible man for a paramour." She produced another order slate with a high-handed flourish and plopped it on the bar in front of him. "Just be sure *these* are ready when I return."

Mistress of the Golden Cords

"Oh, yes, milady! And will you be requiring – what the – *three* bottles of cask aged Phentzino?"

She nodded.

"It's for the dwarven crystal merchants in the northeast corner. Their purse strings were a little tight at first, but I played to their navel and sacral chadakas and they sprang right open."

She made a series of subtle, alluring movements with her hands and hips, demonstrating her magic. The barkeep felt his heart flutter and his his groin stir in response.

"Played to their cha-what-nows?"

"Chadakas. Spinning wheels of energy at different points in the body. Invisible, unless you know how to look."

"More Demian wantcraft?"

"More Demian wantcraft."

Garret realized he was frowning, and willed his stony features to soften. *Come on, you lummox. She found a way to excel at her job, that's all. Don't be such a great, glowering frepp about it.*

"Hey, good for you," he said. "Glad you're getting your money's worth."

"I'll say! My tips have tripled since I started studying the teachings of the goddess. If this keeps up I might actually afford to enroll in university next semester instead of just finagling books out of the library. See you in two drops," she smiled as she tossed her hair in that playful way she always did when they had their private jokes.

Garret had never noticed her tossing her hair that way before they'd become a couple, and he liked to think she'd invented the gesture just for him. He heard her humming as she sashayed through the common room. He recognized the tune: The Song of the Golden Cords from *The Ballad of Demia and Incubaal.* They'd heard it sung by the siren, Kitana, herself at The Pit nearly three weeks prior.

"With golden cords the gods all sought to tie the dancer down. And with golden cords sweet Demia brought their monarch to the ground."

Garret gave his apprentice Farian a nudge and told him he was leaving the bar to retrieve the Phentzino from the wine cellar. The younger barkeep nodded curtly in response, caught up as he was entertaining patrons with his own performance: another sordid story from his past as a Medanite player. Most were regulars who'd heard all his tales several times before, but they guffawed and smacked the counter with the same zeal at all the same parts nonetheless.

"So The Countess Ravenlocke looked at her husband, and with utmost sincerity cried, 'O dearest! Thank the gods you're here! The trow assassin's returned, and look! He's taken the 'guise of the friar!' So before you could say 'cuckolded count' I leapt through the bedroom window, tossed the monk's robes into a fountain, and raced through the courtyard with naught but my smallclothes and a swollen pock-stalk on my person!"

The bar erupted in guffaws and bawdy expletives, and Garret couldn't help but grin as he left the bar and turned down the stairway to the wine cellar. He had to admit, as obnoxious and egocentric as Farian could be, he was a master at charming bar guests, giving the senior barkeep more time to keep the bar stocked and running smoothly.

Garret unlocked the cellar door, glancing as he did at Trina serving the table of dwarven merchants on the far side of the room. She was distributing wine glasses leaning over each dwarf as she did with an arch-backed dip that allowed her golden hair to brush the bearded cheek of each patron, while the rest were treated to an impressive view of her lithe little torso. One of the dwarves, gaping at her in open admiration slipped her a silver coin as he said something that brought the group to a low rumbling chuckle. Trina responded with a quip that made them all burst into oohs, aahs and peals of coarse laughter, as she straightened and smiled down at them.

Then, just as she left to check on the rest of her tables, she tossed her hair in that special way – that way that Garret had thought was just for him. The old barkeep felt a tiny part of him spasm and die.

Turning back to the task at hand, Garret jerked the rickety door open and cursed. No one had lit the lantern – probably another one of Master Wallingtok's cost-cutting measures.

Mistress of the Golden Cords

"Can you be telling me," he could almost hear the proprietor say in his condescending Yllgoni accent, "why I should be paying for burning lamp oil in a room with nobody in it? It's bad for business!"

Sighing, Garret reached into his apron pocket for the flint and striker no self-respecting barkeep should be without, then cursed, as his questing fingers were met with naught but a corkscrew, chalk, charcoal and part of a shriveled brazenberry.

Must have fallen out sometime during the night, he thought, embarassed. *I could go back and ask Farian for his, but, baah, why disrupt the young man's anecdote. I'll just light the lamp with the flint I stashed at the bottom of the stairs.* Confident in his memory of the wine cellar's layout, he edged his way into the stairwell's stygian depths.

As thorough as his memory was, however, it did not encompass the numerous cobwebs that entangled his beard in their musky tendrils. Nor did it cover the newly loosened step that sent him pitching forward into the lightless abyss. Nor the dagger-sized splinter that gashed his hand as he caught the rickety wooden railing to steady himself. By the time he stumbled and cursed his way to the cellar floor and lit the lantern, he felt less a barkeep and more a desperate beast in hunting season: wounded and filthy, with thoughts of murder popping like fireworks in his psyche.

Grinding his teeth, more from anger than pain, he held his hand up to the light and removed the shards of pine from his bloody palm as best he could. He heard laughter from upstairs, thought of Trina's table full of dwarves, and felt an irrational stab to his heart to match the literal piercing of his flesh.

Don't be a fool, he told himself. *Trina's more to you than hair tosses and sexy wiggles, in't she?*

Truth to tell, if in the three moons they'd been dating Trina had proved to be a typical Angelwood vix, more interested in clothing than commitment, Garret would have lost interest by now. But the fact was, she was actually more well-read than anyone he'd ever met, making her conversation as invigorating to his brain as her body was to, well, other parts.

This was why, he told himself, he couldn't get too upset about her interest in Demianism. He was certain it was a purely intellectual exercise. Trina practically lived at the Angelwood University library, and once she got interested in something, she *attacked* it, throwing herself headlong into her research as she did with everything. Just the other day she'd raved about how she'd found an obscure volume of Demian lore called "Light Circles", or some such, for nearly an hour while he'd listened, followed what he could, and wondered what such a brilliant little thing as she could want with a slow lumbering frepp like him.

Now he located and grabbed the three bottles, being careful not to get any blood on the labels, and trudged back upstairs. On his way he heard a boisterous roar from the bar patrons, then another, and then another louder still. The noise brought an ache to his head to match the throbbing sting of his hand.

Pocking Farian and his endless encores, he thought, jaw clenched tighter than ever. *It's closing time. He should be settling those muddlemogs down, not winding them up again!*

On his emergence from the cellar, he saw Farian flipping an empty bottle about with a flaming bundle of dragon's grass stuffed in its spout. He entered the bar and shoved past the apprentice in a musky, blood-spattered fury, thumping the wine bottles down on the service well and shot Farian a baleful glare. The younger barkeep, acknowledged his superior with an impudent wink before making his big finish: taking a mouthful of one hundred fifty proof shusheng and blowing a spectacular fireball before taking another swig of water and simple syrup and extinguishing the makeshift firebrand with his mouth.

"You do remember," Garret grated, grabbing his apprentice's arm with his non-bleeding hand, "that we made last call nigh on half-a-cup ago, and we still have the entire bar to clean and clear if we expect to get out of this place before

Mistress of the Golden Cords

dawn."

"Aye, boss," said Farian, as he rummaged around in the garnish tray with one hand, and his apron pocket with the other. "Couldn't agree more. It's just that Master UiConnall here says he sometimes scouts out opening acts for his troupe and I just wanted to show him my blazing brazenberry trick."

"I don't care if he's the Emperor of Gimadra, if you think I'm gonna cook my kull doing *your* sidework while you – hold a drop! Is that my *striker* you're using?"

"Hmm? Oh, yes. I forgot mine, so I picked your pocket earlier. Old habits, you know. Remind me to give it back when I'm done. Now—" here he turned to the bar patrons as though Garret were no more than his personal stagehand "—observe, ladies and gentlemen, Impresario UiConnall, the common brazenberry, dunked ever so slightly in olive oil—"

"You great pocking kullbung!" Garret snapped. He grabbed the berry out of Farian's fingertips and flung it aside heedless of the disappointed guffaws from the patrons. "Do you have any idea what I just went through in the cellar because of your blackblighted – wait."

A realization struck Garret like a viper. He pulled the junior barkeep aside and hissed in his ear.

"Did you say Impresario *UiConnall?*"

Garret turned to the bar patrons and saw, to his chagrin, a well dressed older gentleman that could only be Shosev UiConnall, owner of the world-renowned Sylvan Guild Repertory Company, as well as uncle and one-time guardian to his lovely paramour. Their eyes locked, and the impresario's narrowed in shrewd perplexity as he tried to determine whether or not he knew this beefy, flush-faced barkeep with cobwebs in his beard. Garret's scalp prickled with flop sweat as he realized his predicament.

Never one to be out of the spotlight for long, Farian stepped between them.

"Impresario UiConnall, may I present our head barkeep, Garret Stockwell. Master Stockwell, may I—"

"I know who he is, you daft bastard!" said Garret, swatting

away his apprentice. "Sir, it's a privilege to meet you. I've been courting, well, your niece and I – we've been – that is to say—"

He thrust out his hand, then quickly retracted it when several droplets of blood from his cut palm spattered across Master UiConnall's fine white cravat and green and gold plaid doublet. The man took in Garret's eccentric behavior with a gracious smile, oblivious to the glistening red flecks now accessorizing his ensemble.

"Well, here now, Garret, is it?" he began to extend a hand then dropped it as Garret flushed, wiped his palm on his apron, winced in pain, and began rummaging under the counter for the bandages in his patch kit. "No need for formality, my man. Truth to tell, Trina and I haven't quite seen – ahem – eye to eye on a number of things for nigh on seven years now. I'm honestly surprised she's said more than two words about me."

"Trina's told me – well, truth to tell, she han't told me much of anything about you. But she did tell me you took her in when her family was trying to marry her off to some lecherous old – well, at any rate that you gave her help and home when she needed it. A gesture for which I know I'll always be grateful. As Trina herself is also, I'm certain."

"Yes, grateful," for the smallest part of an instant, the man's dark eyes tensed in a peculiar expression, that could only be likened to a fox watching a plump chicken from behind a fence – an old rickety fence, with lots of loose boards and fox-sized holes. "Oh posh, it was nothing really. Just a soft-hearted man helping his niece. Anyone would've done the same. But enough of all that. Tell me about yourself, Garret. You must be level-headed and constant as the silver moon to hold young Trina's fancy."

"Well—" Garret grinned sheepishly as he smeared his palm with a finger full of salve and wrapped his hand with practiced precision, "—that sort of thing comes with the job, really."

Relieved beyond words that Trina's uncle was a personable

sort of fellow – as opposed to the stuffy, blue-blooded tyrants the barmaid had always described her parents as being – Garret relaxed into his nightly rituals of wiping surfaces, sealing up garnishes in jars, and returning bundles of herbs to their proper hooks, all the while conversing with the man about each other's businesses. Shosev, proclaiming an interest in opening a small bar connected to the Sylvan Guild Playhouse, listened avidly as Garret talked of vending licenses, permits, and what sort of bribes to offer which councilmen and guild leaders.

Garret, in turn, listened while Shosev explained how he came to own the only all-fairy acting troupe in the Freelands – by purchasing several dozen acres of forest land on the southern edge of the Fertilesand Valley for a wandering tribe of the magical creatures. So long as he owned and helped tend their land, they would provide his audiences with a splendid array of magical entertainment – and a significant crop of high-quality forest-growing nuts and berries to boot.

As if to illustrate his point, the impresario turned and introduced Garret to a man sitting silently to his right, one Faru Oi Saggamai. A man who, now that the barkeep noticed it, was not a man at all but a fairy: wings concealed under a loose-fitting black shirt, upsweeping eyebrows obscured by a silver circlet of asymmetrical leave and twig designs the Fae Folk favored. They clasped wrists in greeting, the fairy's arm reminding him of the tin he'd sometimes worked back in his blacksmithing days – small and delicate, but with great inner resilience.

"So," said Garret conversationally, "how do you like Angelwood's entertainments racket?"

"We have a satisfactory arrangement."

"I'm sure. I know you folk dance to a different beat from the rest of the polis. I once helped cater a First Harvest rite for a tribe in the Canyon of Laurels. The Poplar tribe, you know them?"

"I know of them, yes."

"Well, it was a wild night, *that's* for certain. But I'm sure you know all about that; your tribe must have First Harvest rites of its own, right?"

"No."

The fairy's abruptness surprised the barkeep, putting him at a loss for words. Fortunately, Shosev interceded, "Garret, my fine friend, the thing you must realize about Fae Folk is that diversity is their highest virtue. Every tribe has its own traditions. Master Saggamai here is domenua of the Desert Oak tribe, whose ways are a bit more solemn than most. I remember when I first found them back in Alsyra on the outskirts of the Cynoc wastelands—"

The more Master UiConnall spoke, the more Garret began to admire the man's charm and sophistication. He was slim, but without any sense of encroaching frailty common to men his age. Even his baldness seemed a choice of fashion, rather than a curse of nature, his remaining hair being trimmed to such immaculate precision. Garret, were it not for the constant motion of his hands, was sure he'd be rubbing his own stubbly pate in self-conscious agitation.

"Garret, sweetie, I know it's past last call, but I think I can sell those dwarves another bottle or two of Phentzino to take to their rooms, if—"

Trina flounced up to the service well chittering and glowing at her newfound powers of persuasion, then froze when she saw her uncle. She visibly paled, and for a moment, she seemed another being entirely: some solitary creature that had spent her life hidden in shadow. Garret, sensing he'd fallen in the midst of some unknown family squabble stepped back and began wiping down the back counter. Still, he kept them the uncle and niece in the corner of his eye as though they were belligerent ogres on their ninth tumblers of honey jack.

Noble family, Garret, you great floundering lack-a-wit, why didn't you go let her know her uncle was here? Of course, she comes from a noble family with gods know what subterfuge and squabbles. Pocking abis, what have I got myself into?

"Yes, two more bottles, of course," he said. "Farian, go to the cellar and get two more Phentzinos for Trina."

Mistress of the Golden Cords

Farian, who'd found another brazenberry and was about to retry his bar trick for the two or three patrons that were still halfway interested, looked at him incredulously. "Rather a long time after last call, innit?"

"They'll be taking them to their rooms."

"Still, Master Wallingtok's policy regarding afterhours imbibing—"

"To the 'byss with Wallingtok's policy!" Garret shouted, snatching the berry out of Farian's hand and flinging it into the dump trough. "And to the 'byss with your flaming brazenberries! If you put half as much effort into *tending* this bar as you do into turning it into your personal stage, I could probably open my *own* tavern by now. Now go get those blackblighted wines before I douse *you* with olive oil and see how *you* dance when I set you aflame!"

With that, the master barkeep grabbed his apprentice roughly and propelled him toward the cellar door.

"Yes! Right! Fine!" Farian exclaimed, fighting to maintain his balance and some semblance of dignity. "*You're* the one who's always crackin' *my* kull over not following the rules. And what happened to – ah, shest on a shirttail! That was our last brazenberry! You know, it's hard enough to get an audience with anyone that matters in this town without employers stalkblocking every attempt—"

As Farian fumed and muttered his way down the stairs, Garret turned and saw that Trina had engaged her uncle in some sort of subtle confrontation. She stood, blue eyes smoldering, one hand on the corner of the bar, the other on her hip, while the man sat half-turned on his barstool, a halfsmile pursing his lips as though he were not only fully aware of the awkwardness of the moment, but savoring it's taste as one might a dry Solandische red.

"I'm sorry, uncle," she said in a tone that was anything but, "I've just been so preoccupied with my own success I haven't had time to keep in touch."

"Of *course*, dolly, I completely understand. Hospitality can be a demanding business. Exhausting labor. Long hours.

Loutish patrons. Still, anything's better than what you had to put up with back in Alsyra, eh?"

The comment seemed innocuous, but Trina's face darkened as though she were being strangled.

"Ha," Garret interjected, coming to Trina's defense. If her uncle was implying as he seemed to be that she'd made bad life choices, well, the barkeep had himself dealt with more than his own fair share of disappointed relatives. "That's life in the Freelands, for you. Hustling day and night. Never a penny to your name. But I tell you, folks here wouldn't trade it for anything. It's the thrill that gets you. The excitement of living around so much *possibility!* Why, just the other day, the Siren Kitana herself took Trina aside, waxing lyrical over her great potential."

"Did she?" Shosev exclaimed, "Trina, that's wonderful! I had no idea you were interested in the performing arts! You know you can always use me as a resource. The Sylvan Guild is an all-fairy troupe, of course, but I know several companies that would love to have you. By the Abyss! I could even promote you as a solo act, once we conjured up some material, of course."

"I don't think so, Uncle," she said, glancing at Garret with a dire expression. The barkeep snapped his mouth shut hoping the look was merely a warning and not a curse.

Pocking noble families!

"I've never had more than a passing interest in the arts until recently. And if I *do* decide to walk that path, I wouldn't want people thinking I'd had to rely on nepotism for my success."

"Oh, of course," scoffed Shosev with an eye-roll that took his whole head with it. "Because *no* great performer has ever used *family* connections to get what they want. Watch out for this one, Garret. Her lust for adventure is matched only by her egoism."

"A trait that runs in my family," Trina replied through her teeth.

"Yes, well," he said, rising from his barstool and reaching

Mistress of the Golden Cords

for his coin purse. "You just be careful, young lady. The entertainments business is full of jawdy snollygosters who devour innocent girls like Sunderfest sweetcakes.

"And you, Garret," he continued, pressing a silver mark into the barkeep's palm, "keep the change, and keep a firm hold on my niece. She'll leave you in a lurch to chase a falling star if you're not careful."

"I'll see she stays well, sir." Garret was not entirely sure what the impresario meant, but something about Master UiConnall's tone put his hackles up, and he grabbed Trina's hand protectively. She flashed him a smile that didn't quite reach her eyes and turned away, watching her uncle as though he might at any moment turn into a monster and attack.

"Master UiConnall, wait!" Farian burst into the bar, elbowed past Garret and plunked two bottles of Phentzino down on the bar. "Just a moment of your time, sir, if you please!"

The man rolled his eyes and nodded for the young barkeep to continue. Garret resisted the urge to give his apprentice a clout upside the head.

"And now my friends, without further ado, I give you, *the flaming brazenberry!* You will note that I have, of necessity, replaced the customary brazenberry with a common fuzzberry, yet the principle remains—"

"Ho, fellow! You don't want to do that."

"Nonsense, Impressario! An experienced performer such as I can improvise a way through any complication. Now watch as I first lightly anoint the berry with olive oil—"

The moment the first drop of oil touched the fuzzberry's bristly pink skin, the fruit turned brown and burst open, erupting in a pungent black cloud that filled the common room with a stench like sewers of the Abyss. The bar patrons scattered with guffaws and dramatic groans:

"Leave it to Daringsford to clear a room with *half* a magic trick!"

"Hey, at least it dun't stink as bad as his poetry!"

"You idiot," the impresario laughed, shaking his head.

"Everyone knows fuzzberries react badly to olive oil. I should know: they're the largest crop my grove produces. Don't quit your day job."

"Wait! My real talent is song, anyway. I you'd let me get my—"

"I suspect 'talent' is too strong a term. Sorry, fellow but the folk I deal with only handle the best. I'd recommend East Bentwood Clown School. I'm sure with training you could master a pratfall or two."

As Farian lowered his reddening face, Shosev moved close to Trina for a kiss on the cheek, then lingered there, breast to breast, one hand on the back of the barmaid's head as though it were a plaything.

"Do come and see me soon, my dear," UiConnall hissed into his niece's ear. "I get so lonely in that grand old manse of mine. If you don't visit, I might just have to invite your *parents* to visit the Freelands for a spell. It's been a while since we spoke but I'm sure we could find *some*thing of mutual interest to discuss."

"Master UiConnall, I must protest—" Garret began, but the impresario was already striding toward the door.

The barkeep felt a shiver run through Trina's small hand, so he kissed it and held it in both of his as he wracked his brain for something comforting to say.

As usual, Farian thought it first.

"Bit of a jawdy old lech, in't he?" said the apprentice, tossing the rancid fuzzberry remains in the dump trough and wiping his hand on his apron. "Almost makes me glad I din't get an audition with him. Almost."

"Trina," said Garret, finally finding his voice. "If that was some sort of threat, I'll protect you. You don't have to do anything you don't want to."

"Thank you, Garret," she said, her smile belied by her voice's tightness. "Both of you. But please don't worry yourselves. I've been handling my uncle for longer than anyone. My problems are my own. Now, if you're done being gallant, I've got work to do."

Mistress of the Golden Cords

Quick as a rabbit through a broken fence, Trina slipped her fingers out of Garret's hands. Her table of dwarven crystal merchants were calling, waving rib bones and thumping the table with their flagons. That was the reason the barmaid had rushed away from him in such a hurry, Garret told himself. And that nauseous feeling in the back of his mouth was only from the fumes of putrefying fuzzberry. Only that and nothing more.

Adam Berk

~ IV ~

Farian sang and strummed his lute as the Demian priestesses and novices led their aspirants in laconic circles around the fountains and flowerbeds of the temple courtyard. From the marble dais by the east wall gave the bard enjoyed a splendid view of the area, even if the smooth white stone beneath his boots made him feel a bit like a sacrificial beast on an altar.

The holy women promenaded and preened in their summer finery: sky blue silk sarongs wrapped about them in countless ways, accentuating the countless beauteous varieties of feminine shoulders and breasts, hips and legs. Their guests were every variety of Angelwood denizen: rich and poor, fair and foul, man or woman. Yet every one of them drifted about the yard with the same glittery-eyed grin as the temple staff showered them with flirtatious conversation, touches, and movements honed by their mistresses for greatest libidinal impact. Some movements were so effective Farian had to hold his lute low to conceal a stiffening stalk in his breeches.

I must remember to take my payment in actual money this time, the minstrel thought as he crooned his way through the final verses of the first act of *The Ballad of Demia and Incubaal.*

Mistress of the Golden Cords

Though memories of the so-called *healing rite* he'd taken as payment with a lithe young priestess the week before made him hold his lute lower than ever.

He'd just finished the last verse of the ballad's second movement, when he saw Trina UiConnall being led around a bed of towering white hollyhocks and blue foxgloves by the high priestess, Majjikphima Hilanda. They walked with slow sweeping strides and arrived at the dais just as Farian squeezed off the last sustained vowel of his song, as though their amble were an elaborate dance in itself.

"—must make him understand," the high priestess was saying, "that once you enter the rite, it is not *you* who act, but the goddess of desire who acts *through* you once you surrender your body for her use."

"I understand completely," Trina replied. "I just don't think Garret will see it that way. I mean, he'd like to think that when it comes to my body, he's got first dibs, right?"

"Right. Only he doesn't, does he? It's *you* who has 'first dibs' on your *own* body. None should have more right to enjoy the pleasures of your flesh than you yourself, wouldn't you say?"

"That's a fair point. But you have to admit, most people just don't think like that, do they?"

Mistress Hilanda nodded, a look of regret shading her perfect face as a passing cloud might shade a pristine field of wildflowers.

"It's true. And this you must consider before joining our order. To most of Ardyn, the flesh is no more than a carriage to take them where they want to go, and desire, the horses that pull it. But to us desire is the song of the Great Divine, and our flesh the voice that sings it. Neither scholar, noble, nor worker will ever truly understand your journey."

"Especially," Farian interjected with a grin, "if the worker's a freppish old barkeep who hasn't had a paramour since the Moonflower Purchases."

Trina rolled her eyes, and the high priestess flashed a grin that pierced the bard from heart to groin with its seductive finery. The priestess' eyes were green as the darkest jungles, her full lips moist and inviting as a pond in mid-summer, her teeth as white and gleaming as a wolf's half-a-drop before it bites. Farian could not help but stare and wonder how many ballads he'd have to sing to pay for an hour with so divine a creature as this.

"G'on, Fare!" said Trina. "That's your master you're talking about, you know."

"It is a bard's prerogative," he replied with a bow, "to encompass the gods' truth in words no matter how unflattering they may be."

"No matter if you sound like a total kullbung while doing it?"

"That, milady, is one of the perks of the job."

"You two know each other?"

The high priestess looked back and forth between the two of them with a perfect, arching eyebrow, and a mischievous half-smile that made Farian want to devour her mouth like a sweetmeat.

"We work together," said Trina.

"Interesting. By the cords linking your central chadakas, I'd have thought it more than that."

As the older woman fixed him with a knowing stare, it was all Farian could do to keep from blushing. What the priestess had no doubt intuited was that Farian and Trina had been casually flirting ever since he'd come to work at the Dragonsbane, nine months hence. He'd never allowed it to progress further out of deference (if not always respect) to Garret, his mentor, but there had always been a part of him that wondered if the barmaid would be as lively in coitus as she was in conversation. The same part that wondered even now how she'd look in a sky blue sarong or, more pertinently, *out* of it.

"Alas," said the high priestess, her green, green eyes turning laconically to an older gentleman in a fine blue and white houppelande entering the garden, "we shall have to conclude this pleasant exchange another time. Councilman

Mistress of the Golden Cords

Laschmunn just arrived with what I believe will be a most equitable contract between us and The Pit's board of licensees. Please excuse me."

She kissed Trina on both cheeks, before doing the same to Farian, giving his shoulder a tender little squeeze that nearly made him burst his breeches.

"So you're spending more time at the temple than usual," said the bard to his co-worker. "Could it be that the Dance of the Goddess has pulled you to your feet?"

"Could be," said Trina with a wink and a charming half-smile that didn't quite reach her eyes.

Farian couldn't help but grin as visions of potential healing sessions with the beautiful barmaid cavorted through his brain. The temple's castle-like complex was only a fraction of the Demians' holdings in Angelwood. The Temple of the Cavorting Incarnate also owned dozens of "healing houses" along Veneria, Goddess, and Numa Beaches built at regular intervals all the way up to the southern mouth of Seamount Canyon. There were magically heated springs, wooded yards with fragrant flowers and soft grass, and soft-lit rooms with all manners of cushions and furs, oils and erotic devices.

Picturing Trina's slender body and luminous pale skin in such a setting was a bit jarring – like seeing one's cousin naked. But after the initial shock the idea proved more persistent than most that danced through Farian's capricious mind.

"And what's *that* look for?" asked Trina, her sharp stare bursting his rapacious mental bubble.

"What? Ha! Just thinkin' about the future, dolly. And about how well this place suits your spirit. Perhaps I can visit you some time and we can explore the mysteries of the divine together."

She rolled her eyes. "If that's what the god within leads you to do."

"Oh, he's leading all right. And if I spend much more time thinking about it, I'll have my own compass needle to prove it."

She laughed, but not wholeheartedly, turning as she did

and sitting on the edge of the stone dais. Something about the way she shrugged her shoulders seemed to indicate a need for comfort, so Farian sat next to her, eager to oblige. Until he saw the tears suspended in her eyes.

"Ho, here now, what—? Oh. You haven't told Garret yet, have you?"

"No." The tears fell, then, one after another in tumbling wet dollops down her flushing cheeks. "I just have to find the right words, you know? It's not that I don't – that I don't love him. It's just – well, I guess it's just timing really."

Farian put his arms around her, and she buried her face in his shoulder. As he felt her tears soaking into the fine Gimadran flax of his best shirt, a more complete picture of the barmaid's complicated life formed in his mind.

Well, he thought, *so much for* that *adventure. Sweet Mogu! Why do women have to make sex so complicated?*

He waited for her sobs to pass, then said, "You don't really want to become a Demian priestess, do you?"

She opened her mouth, then froze as though she knew what she was about to say would leave a horrible taste in her mouth.

"The priestesses live good lives here," she said, her tone lowering along with her golden lashes. "Better lives than a lot of others I've known."

Farian grimaced as every salacious thought in his mind turned as unarousing as rotting fuzzberries.

"This have anything to do with that bosky shest with your uncle last night?"

Trina nodded, wiping her eyes with the heels of her hands. "He's threatening to tell my family where I am."

"Ah," said Farian as even more of the girl's background fell into place in his head. "So you're nobility then."

"You're rather quick on the uptake, aren't you?"

"I played with my troupe at enough noble houses back in Medan to know class when I see it. Alsyran nobility are a bit stuffier than Medanite, but their manners are much the same."

"If you say so. My parents had me engaged to marry. The

Mistress of the Golden Cords

old Laird of Leightyn, Cerwyn UiMalleigh, who has more lands than he has teeth."

"At least he shouldn't be a threat to your freedom much longer."

"Because of his age? Bah, from all reports, the old kullbung's so ornery, even death wants naught to do with him. But even if he died tomorrow, I wouldn't go back. My parents fell on hard times, and their solution was to sell me off like a prize cow. All that land and lineage dreff is the stuff of the past. The way it is here in the Freelands with its markets and magic devices and, well, *free*ness – that's the future."

"That's certainly what brought *me* out here," said the barkeep-bard. "Don't think I'd ever trade *my* freeness for a life stuck in some temple, though. No matter *how* much sex I got to have."

"G'on, Daringsford, it's not as bad as all that. There's a spiritual side to it all that just – well, it just makes everything make sense, you know? And anyway, it's better than running again, or trying to fight my uncle."

"Old Shosey's really as powerful as all that, eh?"

"He has the largest estate in the Fertilesand Valley. Half the guildmasters and councilmen in Angelwood are in his pocket, and the other half want to be."

"I figured as much. But that's no reason to think you can't beat him."

"Seems reason enough to me! The man once had a playhouse owner beaten bloody for cancelling a show."

"One thing I've learned from playing for nobility: money and power are double-edged swords. Rich pockers can do a lot more with their wealth than you or I, but they can also have a lot more done *to* them."

Trina looked intrigued. "Such as?"

"Hmm," Farian tapped his chin as his hustler's instincts began listing everything he knew and needed to know about Shosev UiConnal. Next to sex and music, fleecing rich kullbungs was his favorite thing in the world.

"You've still got Corpdays off?"

"Yes."

"Perfect. Give me three days, and I guarantee you I'll find something we can use against the old pockstocker."

"You can't be serious. You're going to risk wigging off one of the most powerful men in Angelwood – for me?"

Farian shrugged. "The man's a pompous kullbung. Bentwood Clown School, he says. I'll show *him* who shouldn't quit his day job! Besides, I don't like seeing good people getting pushed around. A girl like you should be able to do whatever she wants with her life."

Trina's eyes narrowed at this. "A girl like me, huh?"

"Well, ho, come now. You know what I mean."

She stared at him a moment longer until she'd apparently seen him squirm enough, then smiled that same distant half-smile he'd seen before.

"Yeah," she said. "Now that I think about it, I suppose I do."

Mistress of the Golden Cords

~ V ~

"It'll be winter by the time you've picked that byss-blighted lock. Why don't I just smash it with a big rock and be done with it?"

"Because, you great lumbering frollygepp," the apprentice barkeep hissed up at his master from his crouching position by the door, "when you're criminally trespassing on the estate of a ruthless rich pockstalker, you'll want to be as quiet as possible!"

"There's no way anyone can hear us here. We're over two hundred paces away from the main house."

"We're also on the outskirts of a fairy grove, remember? The trees have ears. Literally!"

Funny, thought Trina. *Is this what it's like to have friends? I never thought it'd be so — weird!*

Trina kept watch as Farian and Garret bickered by the locked door of her Uncle Shosev's garden shed, her insides flipping between warm flutters and cold lurches. The barkeeps' efforts and camaraderie filled her with a strength she'd never felt before. She knew she should be grateful for their help, but having them traipsing around the grounds of her former home felt as awkward as finding her kid sister trying on her small clothes.

If she'd ever had a kid sister, that is.

Which was the biggest part of all her problems, now that she thought about it. If she hadn't been an only child, her noble parents wouldn't have had to resort to such desperate measures to save their estate. They could have collected dowries from several minor houses, instead of selling her off at age twelve to the highest bidder – the toothless old Laird UiMalleigh, whose reputation with women was as soiled as his undergarments.

And yet, if she *had* married, even to a noble of her choice, where would she be now? Stuck at the manor house of some Alsyran laird more interested in her land and lineage than he ever would be in her? Whiling away her days, riding, or dabbling in various arts, or managing the household staff, while her husband traveled about securing political alliances at court, drinking at balls, and pocking any pretty serving girl he pleased? Try as she might, she couldn't picture herself in that world anymore.

The lock fell open with a hearty click. Farian did a little dance of triumph while Garret entered the shed and rummaged about, looking for iron: a garden tool, or a weight. Even a nail would do.

The barkeep-bard had spent the day asking a motley assortment of performers, confidence men, and thieves about the terms of a fairy contract, such as the one Trina's uncle had with the members of his Sylvan Guild players. He'd discovered that despite the contracts' many variations, there were always three primary requisites. The keeper of a fairy grove must (A) cause no harm, accidental or otherwise, to any of the vegetation therein, (B) spill no blood upon the forest's soil, and (C) leave no iron within ten paces of the forest's heart. If the four of them could drop a piece of iron owned by the impresario at the appropriate place, Uncle Shossy would soon be too busy serving a sentence as the fairies' indentured servant to cause his niece any more trouble.

Trina heard the sound of heavy breathing behind her and

Mistress of the Golden Cords

turned to find Maggie jogging up to her from the direction of the manse. She was wearing all black like the rest of them – a half-cloak over a tightly corseted evening dress tied off at the waist and partially tucked into what seemed to be workman's breeches. When Trina had asked where the older barmaid had got a man's pantaloons, Maggie had winked and promised to tell her the story later.

"Right," she huffed. "Didn't see any new guard houses or barracks. Grounds were just like you said. One main house. One guest house. Groundskeeper's shanty, stables, mill, and smithy."

"Thank the gods," said Trina. "He probably hasn't hired any new house guards or stavemen then. I told you before, Uncle Shosev was never much for hiring security. You didn't need to go skulking around like some trow elf assassin. What would you have done if you were caught?"

Maggie shrugged. "I dunno, probably told 'em I was a newly hired servant what got lost on the way to the privy. Better I get caught than you."

"Better *no* one gets caught! My uncle doesn't deal with law enforcement unless he has to. If someone saw you, a year's forced servitude for trespassing would be the *best* thing that could happen."

"Guess I won't get caught, then."

Trina threw up her arms in surrender. "Why you're even out here in the first place is beyond me."

Maggie's freckled cheeks dimpled in a puzzled half-smile. "I'm here 'cause you're my friend, you're in trouble, and you've got naught but two stalk-bridled, bung-brains for assistance. Din't you ever pull no capers like this with your friends back in Alsyra?"

"No."

I didn't have friends back in Alsyra.

The thought made her ache inside, and before she knew it she'd thrown her arms around Maggie's ample chest in a tight hug. She might never have had a sister, Trina reflected, but if she could somehow choose one, right then she knew her choice would be Maggie UiCrielvan.

"All right, now," Maggie chuckled, patting her arm. "Best we get on with things now. The boys are coming back."

Trina looked and saw Garret and Farian bounding toward them from the shed. Garret carried an edging iron: a heavy half-moon blade on a hickory pole that would seem awkward and unwieldy in a smaller man's hands.

"Think this'll have to do," said the larger barkeep holding the blade up to the moonlight. "It's Gai-Autische steel which is as close to pure iron as you get these days. The giants that worked it used barely any carbon or alloys at all. Excellent craftsmanship, though."

Trina smiled, remembering Garret's past as a blacksmith. Was there anything the man didn't know? Any task he couldn't perform? The thought made her feel more than a little helpless by comparison.

Exchanging nervous glances and excited whispers, the four of them retrieved their lanterns from where they'd stashed them at the forest's edge. After ensuring the shutters were properly closed, they lit the wicks, kneeling in a circle to hide the sparks, exchanged another round of furtive expressions, and entered the fairy grove.

As soon as her feet hit the loamy path, Trina noticed a strange restlessness in the air. She'd walked through her uncle's faewood many times in her younger years, but did not remember it ever feeling so agitated. At first she thought it was only the thrill of their criminal trespass, but as they went deeper, she noticed the desert oak, maple, and eucalyptus leaves trembling ever so slightly, despite the stillness of the warm summer air.

Both moons were out tonight: Luminaria's silver light and Shaydawen's deep blue glow trickled through the leafy canopy above, imbuing the surrounding trunks, roots, and branches with pale green-blue iridescence. As they made their way deeper into the faewood, even this light diminished until only the faintest outlines of their backs and shoulders were visible in the gloom. Finally, Garret stopped, placing the edging iron on

Mistress of the Golden Cords

the ground, and opening his lantern's shutters. Trina and the others followed suit. He looked at her and, with a wide-eyed look that made her think of a loyal hound on a day-hike, nodded signaling that she should take the lead.

Trina smiled back, patting the big man's chest – so warm and solid under her delicate fingers – and moved to the front of the group. It had been over seven years since she'd set foot in the grove, and she didn't recall ever doing so at night, but she was certain she could lead them to the forest's heart. The winding path narrowed as they walked until they had to move in single file, ducking and swaying around the leafy branches and brambles prodding them from either side. The path forked once, twice, then thrice, and Trina led them down the left, right, and left branch without delay. She knew if she stopped to think, even for a moment, she would second guess herself and get them all lost.

The flickering lantern light illuminated her surroundings in sporadic bursts, as vegetative scenes and memories jumped and flared to life around her. There were the twisted limbs of the oak she'd climbed the first time she'd ever worn a shirt and breeches instead of some stifling lady's dress. There was the little glade filled with leaves, catkins and eucalyptus bark where she'd had her dalliance with her first love, Mahti the stable boy. There was the slowly crumbling stump of a lightning-blasted old maple where she'd sat and wept after the first time Uncle Shosev had—

Suddenly, she stumbled forward as an oak root caught her foot. Catching herself in a few lurching steps, she held up her hands, hoping her companions saw the gesture before they crashed into her in a noisy jumble. But no one did. No one bumped her.

Or touched her.

Or even reached her side.

Perplexed by the surrounding stillness, she turned about, holding her lantern high. Her breath caught in her throat. She saw no sign of her companions. Or even the path they'd been walking on. A surge of panic shot through her as she peered this way and that into the surrounding darkness, finding only the uncaring trunks of Eucalyptus and Greatflower trees, pale and unyielding as prison bars.

"We have been waiting for you, sweetling child."

The words seemed to come from every direction at once – before, behind, and even within so they seemed to buzz in her bones. They were soft as the summer air, pervasive as the blood in her veins, and familiar as a childhood scar. Taking a deep breath she lowered her lantern and calmed her nerves as best she could.

"We knew that you'd return to us in time, but you must be in desperate need indeed to bring the black-burning iron to our halls."

Shest! she thought. *This is bad.*

This time the voice came from just behind her ear. She turned to face the speaker: the fairy domenua, Faru Oi Saggamai. He looked much the same now as he did back at the Dragonsbane, same severe mouth and delicate features. His clothing, however, was much improved – a tunic that shimmered green as a jade beetle's shell, polished silver jewelry that adorned his face and hands in odd places, and a shirt, breeches and boots of an indeterminate color that blinked in and out of sight the faint moonlight. His expression held a vibrant intensity she'd never seen before. His pale skin shone, his eyes glowed, and his wings, no longer the small wilted things concealed under his shirt, spread wide behind him, radiant as polished copper.

Immediately, she fumbled her way into the posture of supplication she'd learned long ago from her uncle – heels together, feet angled away from the fairy, palms out in an opening gesture spreading outward from just below her navel. The domenua studied her critically, then gave a curt nod. Trina shifted into a more natural position, though whether the fairy chieftain was signifying approval of her manners, forgiveness of her trespass, or something deeper, she could not say.

"*Sello ah sreichito,* Domenua," she said, the greeting one of

Mistress of the Golden Cords

the few fairy phrases she remembered. "Please don't be angry with us. We didn't mean any harm, we only –"

"You only sought to bring poison to our land, and deceive us so we'd imprison our honored host."

Blood and ashes, we are so pocked!

Trina hung her head, fighting all the while to keep the sudden storm of panic now swirling through her head from blowing away her composure.

"Please, Domenua. Forgive us."

She raised her face as she spoke, slow and wide eyed, unthinkingly falling into an expression the Demian priestesses called, *yearning-to-touch-the-sunset*. The fairy chieftain raised a sweeping eyebrow in response.

An idea came to her. Remembering her lessons from the temple, Trina took in the domenua's posture at a glance, noting the dominance of his root, chest, and brow chadakas.

"I know we should have come to you first," she continued, lips parting in the charming smile of *honey-on-my-lips-and-fingers* as she let her body fall into the *fumbling-sweetcakes* posture. "It's just, I know you and your people don't like dealing with us bumbling humans any more than you have to. It's bad enough you have to deal with my *uncle* as much as you do."

Saggamai stared at her, his face unreadable. Trina felt her smile growing forced, so she gave a nervous laugh and allowed her face to fall into *waking-on-a-chilly-morning*, while visualizing a golden cord linking her right hand to the fairy's chest chadaka.

The domenua blinked twice, looking at her quizzically for a moment before bursting into laughter. The sound was sudden enough to make the barmaid jump, and had a wildness in it that made her feel as though the ground beneath were slowly crumbling.

"So you *have* been studying with the Demian clerics," said the fairy. "I thought I saw Jane Forecroft's handiwork!"

Trina felt as though an ox yoke had just been dropped onto her shoulders. Feeling her face fall, she considered trying *caught-rescuing-a-kitten*, then thought better of it. She remembered one of the few times she'd encountered the domenua while living with her uncle. Mahti had stolen some wild honey for her – at *her* provocation now that she'd thought of it – from one of the fairies' sacred hives, and she'd tried to lie on his behalf. Saggamai had seen through deception immediately, had turned Mahti into a badger for two months, and had given her the ears of a donkey for a fortnight.

So the barmaid decided honesty was her best and only chance.

"I'm sorry, Domenua. But I can't have Shosev telling my parents where I live. And I certainly can't go back to being his – whatever it was he tried to make me."

"Property," said the fairy.

Trina met his bright green eyes and saw the cool hardness of an Alsyran oak in winter. But there was something else there as well – a certain tension in his smooth brow and thin lips. Could it be sympathy?

"The shade of your bloom has yet to show, dear child," Saggamai continued. She didn't flinch from his gaze, though it felt as though it were infiltrating every part of her. "You're an infant squirrel that yearns to leave its nest. But the branches you would walk are wind bestirred, and the jaws of the beasts below are sharp and swift. And whether the Green One wills you to mature? Well, that question we'll now answer. Come."

There was something about the fairy's manner when he turned that seemed to pull Trina along with him. In the dim light she couldn't tell if there was a path beneath her feet or not. His iridescent wings were the only things she could see clearly, so she focused on them. They were astoundingly flexible, she noted, swelling and diminishing like the leaves of a plant, bending and twisting to stay out of reach from the branches and vines emerging from the darkness on all sides. He spoke as he walked, his speech flowing with the rhythm of his steps and the growing and wilting of his coppery wings.

"Those Demian arts you learn are not unique, child. They borrow much from fairy songs and lore. They're based on arts which we call Weaving Glamour, which helped us craft our music from the wild."

Mistress of the Golden Cords

The shapes of trunks and leafy boughs emerged from the gloom as the forest lightened, though whether it was from thinning foliage, impending dawn, or her own eyes adjusting to the dark she could not say. The trees were larger here, the trunks of the maples growing wide as carriages, their lowest limbs high above their heads. In the distance she noticed an amber flicker that she soon recognized as lantern light – the light of *several* lanterns she realized in chagrin, not just the small, shuttered flames of her friends'.

"The golden chords we weave," the fairy continued, "are strains of harmony, combined to celebrate life's abundant song. But the Cult of the Dancer remade them as cords of artifice with which to bind all people to its ways."

But Trina was only half listening. As they came to the outskirts of a clearing the fire lit sight of her captured friends filled her view. A dozen fairy warriors stood, paced, and crouched around them. At least, she thought they were warriors. They held swords, spears, and weapons she didn't even know the name of. Their armor, clothing, and physiques were so diverse they might have been blacksmiths or basket weavers for all she could tell. One wore a shirt of shining red scale mail of such delicate craftsmanship that it might have been made of feathers. Another had a robe of translucent fabric that shone like silk, yet hung heavy about her small, dark limbs, as though it were weighted with unseen iron. And still another was clothed so completely in tree bark that he appeared to be made of the stuff.

Then her uncle entered the clearing, and the full truth of her predicament hit home. They were caught! The fairies would press her friends into servitude for their criminal trespass, while Shosev would subject her to such perversions as only the oldest gods could know. Despair rising inside her, she lunged forward with murderous intent.

But the fairy domenua caught her by the arm.

"And what do you intend to do here, child?"

"I don't know. Smash him upside his mog with my lantern? Beg for mercy?"

Saggamai pursed his lips and shook his head.

"Use the power with which you have been gifted." He spoke slowly as a parent instructing a willful toddler. "You know enough to change the world at will. Find the source that feeds desire's river, and life itself will rise to heed your call."

The fairy released her arm and gave a dismissive wave, motioning that she must go and do whatever it was she was supposed to do. Trina's head spun. Find the source of desire's river? What in the Abyss was that supposed to mean? This was no time for riddles! Her uncle was about to do gods knew what to her friends and she was powerless to prevent it!

Use the power with which you have been gifted. You know enough to change the world at will.

Did he mean Demian wantcraft? If she plied the dance of the golden chords on her uncle it just might work. But gods! The thought of it brought up memories she'd long since tried to carve out of her mind.

She had lied to Maggie about her and her uncle's relationship. The part about beating him off with a bed warmer was true. But the part about that being the *only* night he had come to her bed was *not*.

And how *could* she tell her friend what had truly happened? How could the two of them ever just flob about when every time Mags looked at her she saw her for what she truly was: the trash receptacle for her uncle's abominable desires. No, like it or not, there would always be a distance between her and the normal world. There would always be that dirty, deformed part of her that could never be set right, and the best she could do was keep it hidden.

Until now.

Okay, Trina. Keep breathing. Naught to do but seduce my own rot-pocking rapist.

She separated her mind from her body trying to perceive her slender limbs, shapely torso and attractive face as nothing more than instruments of her craft. The detachment came surprisingly easy; in one way or another she'd been doing it all her life.

Mistress of the Golden Cords

Drawing herself up into the strong confident posture of *walking-with-a-dragon-at-my-back*, she entered the clearing.

"Hello, Uncle. I see you've met my friends."

Shosev UiConnall turned and looked her over with eyes like frozen tar. The lantern light shone off his smooth scalp and cast heavy shadows about his nose and the cords of his neck, making him resemble a well-dressed vulture.

"Hello, sweetling. I caught your friends bringing iron into my fairy grove. And you too, since I'm sure this whole escapade was your idea."

The sound of his husky arrogant voice stirred unwanted memories. They flew into her head, battering the screen of her sanity like angry hornets. Those thin-fingered hands grabbing her, pinning her down. Those thin, wet lips sliding over—

She slammed a door shut in her mind, focusing all her attention on controlling her breathing and perfecting her craft.

"Oh, uncle," she approaching the impresario with a sultry swagger, "I can see how you might think that. Our last meeting took me by surprise. I'm sorry if I didn't seem as receptive as I might have. I wasn't truly myself."

"Ah. And who were you when you assaulted me with that bed warmer?"

You talk of assault!

A child's voice screamed deep inside her. But she kept her eyes bright and her smile wide and inviting.

"Those were the actions of a – well, of a frightened child. I think you'll find I've grown since then."

She walked up to Shosev, just close enough for him to catch the scent of her perfume (what the Demians called "grasping distance"), then abruptly turned to Garret. The big barkeep was on his knees between two fairies with his arms bound behind him. He glowered at her darkly, and she averted her eyes, praying he could somehow discern what she was doing.

"The plan was this one's," she said, touching Garret's shoulder and giving it the lightest of affectionate squeezes. "When I told him my plans to take you up on your generous offer, he got jealous. When I told him about our past together, he grew enraged and concocted a plan with these other two to leave some of your iron in the faewood."

"Thus violating my fairy contract," he said, moving to stand next to her as she looked down on her bound companions, "putting me in their service and out of your life for years."

"Exactly."

"And I am to believe," he said as he took her by the arm and turned her to face him, "that you do *not* want me out of your life."

That grip again. No! Gods help me I can't do this! It's too pocked! Too wrong!

It took all her will not to struggle. Panic clutched her chest, squeezing all the air from her lungs.

"Uncle Shosey," her voice quivered in the faint whimper of a frightened animal. But the Demians had a way to use that as well. "I'll admit," she said turning to him with the bashful expression and inviting posture of *you-found-my-secret-sweet-now-share-it-with-me*. "It took me a long time to accept the – unusual facets of our relationship. But now that I have, I must say, it intrigues me."

She forced herself to breathe, then relaxed in his grasp, bringing her other hand to rest lightly on his forearm. She visualized her golden cords, emerging from her chest and solar plexus to wind around his three lowest chadakas.

"I do want to be more than just a serving wench," she continued. "You are the wisest, most charming, most perfect man I've ever known, and I would value your guidance above all else. And not just in my career—"

She turned languidly in his grasp sliding her fingers up his arm to his chest.

"—but also in, well—"

She lowered her voice to a warm, throaty purr, moving just close enough for him to feel her breath on his lips.

"—me."

The cords pulled tight. She felt Shosev's body shudder as

Mistress of the Golden Cords

he exhaled. His eyes burned with a fierce, irrational need, and she knew with grim satisfaction that he was in her thrall.

Out of the corner of her eye she glimpsed her friends' faces. Farian's jaw was on his chest. Garret's scalp had turned the darkest shade of crimson she'd ever seen. Maggie looked like she was going to throw up.

The cords shuddered, their grasp on Shosev growing slack. *They hate me.*

The thought took her by surprise. It bore through her, leaving utter emptiness. Her friends – her only friends – had seen her hidden filth, and they hated her for it!

"Oh, Little Cat," said her uncle, using that pet name she so detested, "it thrills me so much to hear those words from your lovely little mouth."

The cords trembled again, more violently this time.

"There's only one thing."

The cords slipped and fell off entirely.

"I don't believe you."

Shosev released her, stepping backward and giving a quick nod to the fairies at her back. Hands grabbed her from behind, pulling her arms back and binding them with thick grass ropes. Something struck the back of her legs, driving her to her knees. And there she stayed, dew from the mossy loam seeping into her skirts.

"Faru Saggamai!" her uncle called out to the surrounding woods. "Get out here, you dour-faced cockalorum. I know you've been watching all this!"

Trina pulled against her bonds, but they held fast. A chill sweat trickled down her face, and between her shoulders. Her chest grew tighter and tighter and the forest began to spin around her.

"Tell me, domenua," Shosev continued, "what is the penalty for bringing iron into a faewood?"

She tried to remember her lessons but they fell away as she clutched at them with her frantic mind. She closed her eyes, tried to slow her breathing, but still the world spun. Like a wheel on a runaway carriage. Like an eye mage's zoetrope, showing the scene of her capture over and over and over. Like a—

Like a chadaka! she realized.

And that's when the craziest idea she'd ever had danced into her brain.

"Twenty years confined to the faewood's bound" said the fairy, answering her uncle. "Naught to eat nor wear but what we give. Naught to do but serve the fae court's whim."

Trina opened her eyes and visualized the ground beneath her knees as a spinning wheel of white light – the crown chadaka of Ardyn, the world itself. She reached out with her own energy, and could almost see the golden cords flowing from points at her head, throat, torso, and groin. She connected the cords to the spinning wheel beneath her.

And the world exploded into life!

"Mm. Interesting. And what about *my* rights to her?"

"As patron all we have belongs to you. Our thrall she'd be, and yours to use as well."

The words skittered across the edge of her consciousness as pure white joy erupted inside her like a fountain. She threw back her head and laughed. Shosev paused still a picture of composure, a spasm of surprised blinks the only betrayal of his disconcertion.

"Dear sweet Uncle!" she cried.

She was window to all the light in the universe, a flying piece of debris in the maelstrom of her mind, scarcely knowing what the next word to spill from her mouth would be.

"You poor foolish man. Iron was only part of the plan! Garret and the others brought blight worms and blackrot beetles to infest this grove. They brought them in jars and released them in those fuzzberry bushes over there."

Shosev and Saggamai turned, her sudden outburst catching both their attention. Her uncle's face was one big disbelieving smirk, the fairy's unreadable as always. She did not care.

Such power as she'd never felt before coursed through her in a euphoric rush. She could *see* Shosev's chadakas – each a consecutive color of the rainbow – arrayed at seven points

Mistress of the Golden Cords

from his groin to the top of his head. But as she reveled in her newfound magic, the rising tide of despair came creeping back. Although she could see her uncle's astral energies, bound as she was she had no way to capture them with her movements.

"We brought the means to kill the beetles as well," she continued, trying to work her wantcraft with smiles, pouts, and shrugs alone. "You can have it if you let us go. Come now, Uncle, I know we've had our differences, but I truly do want no ill will between us. Less than that even, if you take my meaning."

She tried for a partial version of *honey-on-my-lips-and-fingers,* though it felt awkward and forced from her kneeling and bound position. Still, she saw her uncle's lower chadakas flicker as he cast an annoyed glance over his shoulder at the fuzzberry bush.

"I see no beetles. Enough of this nonsense. Domenua Saggamai, throw these lackwits in jail, or whatever vegetative nonsense you preening poofies have for a prison!"

Hands grabbed her upper arms and pulled her to her feet. A geyser of panic surged inside her, blending incongruously with the beatific fluttering sensations of mother Ardyn's great swirling chadaka. She could have succumbed to her fear – let it wash away her will in its desperate current.

But instead she heard the voice of the fairy domenua. *Find the source that feeds desire's river, and all of life will rise to heed your call.* And so she closed her eyes, shutting out the tyranny and doom of the world without, and surrendered to the mysterious spinning lights that danced behind her eyes.

She heard singing first. A beautiful voice: soft yet resonant, carrying through the trees around her as easily as a birdsong or a breeze. After several moments, she realized it was her own.

She opened her eyes to see everyone – her friends, their fairy guards, even her Uncle Shosev – staring at her in rapt abandon. Sound poured from her mouth of its own accord: words in a language she did not recognize. It sounded like fairy, but much, much older. She sang, somehow knowing each perfect syllable to follow its preceding. It rose to a crescendo, until she hit and sustained a piercing strain – atonal and jarring, yet with a *right*ness to it all the same.

The sound made her uncle stagger back as though pierced by an arrow. His chadakas turned to guttering candles, his mouth went wide, and the cords on his neck quivered like newly struck lute strings. His head jerked about, his eyes bulging at terrifying visions only he could see.

"Gods and demons! They're everywhere! Beetles! Blood and ashes, all these pocking, black-blighted beetles! Trina! Tell me the treatment before they ruin me!"

"Release us and I will."

"Of course, of course! Let them go, you fairy fools! Now quick! Tell me what I need to do!"

"The lamps," she said. "They're filled with castor oil. Fatal to blackrot beetles."

"Yes, yes! Of course, of course!"

He ran about in a wild-eyed fury, opening the oil compartments in their lanterns and dousing every branch, leaf, and berry he could find.

Trina felt Garret's big hand rest lightly on her shoulder, followed by Maggie and Farian joining her on either side.

"I guess switching the lamp oil *was* a good idea," said the burly barkeep beside her.

She nodded, grabbing his thick warm fingers as her euphoria faded, as though they were a cable tow back to reality.

"Olive oil is more costly, and doesn't burn as well, but it *does* have its uses."

Shosev drenched the fuzzberry bushes with the oil, and then flew backwards as the vegetation erupted in a smoky, flatulent burst. The impresario landed unceremoniously on his rump, and stared at the smoldering shrubbery as though it were his very life going up in smoke – as indeed it was.

The fairies moved silently to where he sat and surrounded him, each one different from every other, each with a long, coiled rope dangling from their hands. Now that Trina got a good look at the bindings, she noticed they were shimmering

Mistress of the Golden Cords

gold.

"Wait! Saggamai, you can't be serious. Sure, I might have damaged a few berries, but I saved the bush from a swarm of beetles. You *saw* the beetles, didn't you? Saggamai! You pocking savages, our contract still holds! You hear me? The contract holds!"

They closed ranks around the struggling man, and vanished into the fetid fog of rotting fuzzberries.

The stench soon became overwhelming, and Trina and her three companions hastened to what they hoped was the path out of the faewood, stumbling over each other's feet in the now darkened forest. Soon the way grew easier as the canopy thinned, and the light of the two moons once again illuminated the pale trunks of angelwoods, the fluttering leaves and peeling bark of eucalyptus, and the long, reaching branches of desert oaks, twisting through it all like the veins of some great animal.

When they at last emerged, the horizon glowed yellow, turning the sky from black to ashen blue. They found themselves on a small grassy ridge that not even Trina recognized. It overlooked most of her uncle's estate: the handful of small huts and cottages for his personal craftsmen, groundskeepers and other small-folk, the fenced off patches of his vineyard, vegetable gardens, and lemon grove, and the palatial, adobe walled manor house looming in the distance. The early morning light gave the scene a monochrome appearance, colors slowly bleeding into the plants and buildings as the first rays of sunlight peaked over the distant hills.

"Funny how turned around we got, innit?" quipped Farian. "I don't even remember going uphill, do any of you?"

"That *is* weird," said Maggie. "Seemed to me like we went out the same way we went in. How do you suppose that happened?"

"Because I wanted it to."

The group turned in time to see Faru Oi Saggamai emerge from a tangle of leafy boughs and shadows. The fairy domenua appeared smaller than he had in the forest – he'd folded his splendid wings so they resembled a light cloak. Nonetheless, he approached them with an authoritative air, imparting the unspoken reality that he could set the winds themselves against them, if he so chose.

"There's still the matter," he said, shadows of gods-knew-what shifting in the woods behind him. "Of the poison iron. The penalty that must be paid is clear: that you and your companions serve the faewood for a span of time no less than twenty years."

All of them protested at once. Garret exclaimed that he'd carried the iron into the wood, so he alone should pay the consequence. Maggie yelled at the domenua, saying Trina was only acting out of desperation, and if Saggamai couldn't understand that, he was a "useless poofy frepp with an oak twig up his bung!" And Farian tried to calm them both down so he could work out some kind of deal.

Only Trina was silent – mortified at the awful fate she'd inflicted on her former friends. *Still* her friends she marveled. Even after all this they were trying to defend her! It made her sick. They'd seen her with her uncle – seen how soiled and pocked she truly was. How could they still think her worth defending?

"It is also law," said the domenua, holding up a hand for silence, "to gift in kind. Trina's deeds, though harmful they may be, resulted in our wretched patron's capture. And him we've wanted for some time to spurn, as he's profaned our rites in human markets and taken more of our harvest than he's earned. As boon for this reprieve, you're free to leave."

Garret, Maggie and Trina swapped puzzled looks as they mulled over the fairy's flowery words.

"He says," said Farian. "They'll overlook the iron thing because Uncle Shossy's a thieving kullbung they've wanted to imprison for a long time."

As one, they exhaled their relief in sighs and giggles. Domenua Saggamai, apparently satisfied with his proclamation, turned and vanished into the faewood. As the sun slowly rose, the four of them carefully made their way down to steep slope

Mistress of the Golden Cords

toward the imprisoned impresario's property.

"Sure have an odd way of talking, don't they?" said Maggie.

"That's because it's metered," Farian replied. "Music comes as easily to the fae as breathing. Domenuas speak in pentameter, administrators and courtiers in tetrameter, and artisans in trimeter. Faolyr's right next to Medan, you know. I've always wanted to go there."

Farian prattled on to the barmaid as they reached the foot of the slope and headed toward the manor house. Hopefully, Trina was still well liked enough with the staff that they'd lend them a carriage. It was a long walk back to all of their flats from the Fertilesand Valley, and they doubted the harkey coach they'd taken to its outskirts last night was still around.

As they walked, Garret and Trina fell back a pace to talk in private.

"I hope you know," she said. "Whatever I said back there was to get Shosev to let you go. Nothing more."

"Of course," said Garret, putting his arm around her.

She winced in spite of herself. For some reason the sensation of his big meaty weight made it difficult to breath. She'd never minded it before – she loved the gentleness of Garret's touch despite his size, and the way he shortened his stride to better match hers – but now all she felt was a need to crawl under a bush somewhere and die.

"It's just," she said, as she pulled his arm off her back and took his hand instead. "Things got really pocked up – when I was living at my uncle's manor. He did things to me. We did things –"

--that left me broken and empty and feeling like my insides were made of slugs!

She wanted to say it, but couldn't get the words out.

"I understand," said Garret. He kissed her hand, his goatee feeling like how she'd always imagined a bear's fur would feel. "He hurt you. I remember when my da used to hurt me and my sisters. Sometimes you have to do pocked things when you live with someone who hurts you."

It didn't always hurt though.

And that was the worst of it! The times when her own body had betrayed her and taken pleasure in the midst of Shosev's violation and pain. This was the ultimate feeling of powerlessness. She would never – *could* never allow herself to feel anything like that again.

That was something, sadly, that Garret for all his compassion could never understand. It put a distance between the two of them that she worried could never be bridged.

The path to the manor house was long and wound through an orange grove and a field of Gimadran bread corn. The sun continued to rise, slowly warming the cool, dry air. They walked in a silence that was comforting if not cheerful.

Trina's thoughts turned, as they walked, to the confrontation in the faewood. Her desperate attempt at wantcraft hadn't worked – how could it when she'd only been studying a few weeks! All the past trauma it had brought up should have driven her mad but, strangely, it hadn't. On the contrary, she now found herself able to look at past events with a clarity she'd never had before.

Or maybe never allowed herself to have.

It was that light, she realized. That great divine presence that had given her a voice and given that voice power! But was the light healing her or just changing her into something different?

As the four of them came to the manor's entrance, the thought occurred to her that the only way she'd ever know the answer would be to complete her training at the Temple of the Cavorting Incarnate. Shosev's manor was an enormous building with a gleaming white porch adorned with ornate columns. As they mounted the steps, Trina realized just how filled the place was with painful memories – memories that wound through her psyche like spiderwebs, binding and tangling everything she did.

She had to grow until she was big enough to break those cords. Whether Garret or anyone else understood it or not, that was the most important thing she would ever have to do.

Mistress of the Golden Cords

Adam Berk

A Note From the Author

Hail, travellers! I hope you enjoyed your visit to this small corner of Ardyn: the world that lives in my head. If so, you'll be glad to know there are many more stories on the way, each more thrilling than the last.

"But when?" you might ask. "This one was fun, but rather short. I want epics filled with high adventure, characters I know better than my drinking buddies, and exotic lands so vividly described, I can visit them just by closing my eyes!"

Well, my friend, I'd like nothing better than to churn out my tales at break-neck speed, putting into words the countless novels, novellas, novelettes, shorts, and scripts roiling about my addled brain. The thing is, for that to happen, I'll need to stop tending bar 40 hours a week and turn crafting fine, fantastic fiction into a full-time career.

"Ho boy," you might groan, "Now comes the part where he hits me up for money!"

No, dear reader, direct contributions are only one small way you can help. The following list includes options for longer lasting, less costly contributions to my growing creative universe:

- Leave a review on Amazon, Goodreads, or any other site people read. I'd prefer it if you said good things, of course, but any press is good press and any feedback will be obsessed over.
- Like and follow me on social media. That's @AdamBerkWriter for Twitter, Adam Berk (Writer) on Facebook and my website is adamberkwriter.com. I also have a YouTube channel at youtube/c/adamberkwriter.
- Lend a book to a friend. Nothing makes you look cooler than being in the know about alternative media. And, friend, I'm as alternative as they come! So don't

Mistress of the Golden Cords

boggart that literature, man! Pass me around, share me with friends, then get together over beer, liquor, or lattés and laugh about the Freelands' latest insanity.

- Get on my mailing list! Contact me at adamberkwriter.com and send me your email. I'm a bit erratic when it comes to putting out newsletters, so it might be a while before you hear from me, but this is still the second best way to get insider information on upcoming projects, the first being –
- -- Patreon.com! Okay, there it is. If you have a little something extra burning a hole in your pocket, send a donation through patreon.com/adamberk, and I'll do my best to reward you with inside info and Ardynian easter eggs. Who knows, maybe I'll even write a story about you!

And so, fellow travellers, I thank you most sincerely for your presence and patronage of the world of my dreams. I hope our journey together will be a long one filled with laughs, thrills, and hidden wisdom. And, as I say to all my regulars, drive safe, and come back soon!

Sincerely,
your writer and barkeep,

Adam Berk

Appendix

A Guide to Freelandish Slang

And Other Terms

Abis - Same as Abyss, but pronounced AH-bis. The Freelandish word for hell. Portmanteau word combining the Trophican "Abyss" with the Syndraxan *Ajasi* (pron. AH-ja-see).

Abyss – aka the Great Abyss. Place of punishment for evil souls upon their death according to Trophican Ardainite and Evanescicle religions.

Adder - also *Addah*. The male organ as great, large or massive. From the Gimadran word Adpha, meaning great, greatness or phallus.

Brahda – A term of endearment. Same usage as "brother", although for a friend instead of a literal relative. From the Gimadran *brao dong* meaning family friend.

Bosky - Shady, nefarious. From the Old Trophican word for wooded.

Byss-pit - A "hell-hole", or an unpleasant place to work,

Mistress of the Golden Cords

reside, etc. From the words Abyss and pit.

Byss-blighted – Same usage as goddamned. rel. byss-blasted, byss-buggered, or byss-pocked.

Blackrobe – Term of contempt for an entertainments business professional, referencing the black robes commonly worn by Lascivian Mages. E.g. "I wanted a spectacular battle scene in my play, but the pocking *blackrobes* said we didn't have the budget for it."

Blatherrach – Literally, one who assaults others with blather. A person given to voluble, empty talk.

Bucket - Common word for chamber pot, i.e. "in the bucket" which is to say, "down the drain".

Buckethead – One who, metaphorically speaking, has a chamber pot where his brains should be.

Bung - Same usage as "asshole", more commonly in reference to the anatomical part than the type of person (who would more commonly be called a "kullbung").

Cestodal Grafting Imbuement (CGI) – Magecraft term for the process of infesting a performer with magically enhanced tine worms to make the subject heal faster and able to attach severed appendages.

Collywallies - Feelings of nervous apprehension. From "colic" and the Trophican term, collywobbles.

Collywald - A coward. One who is prone to "getting the collywallies".

Chucking Buckets - Term for one who is violently enraged. Originated with the famously insane Angelwood Polis Councilman John Hedwig, who after being cheated by a whore in a hotel suite, began throwing chamber pots about the place in a fit of rage.

Chirk - to cheer (usually followed by "up"). Also, a shrill, chirping noise.

Chirkyjerk - An annoyingly cheerful person.

Chop - to banter, usually in an argumentative way, i.e. "just choppin' ya 'bout."

Clopper - Racial slur for centaur. More commonly used in the Mystican Countries, especially Medan.

Cockalorum - a self-important little man.

Cup – Fifty drams, two thousand five hundred drops, or 0.694 of an hour. There are 36 cups in a day, which is divided into quarters of nine. i.e. "three cups past dawn" is about 8 in the morning, and "eight cups past noon" is around 6 in the evening.

Danglestalk – Literally a man who is impotent. A man who is dull, boring, and/or lacking sex-drive.

Dapper - a waiter, or male servant. Aberration of dapifer.

Dim Dolly – Ditz or bimbo. A scatterbrained woman.

Dolly - A casual term of endearment, used mostly in the Angelwood entertainment industries. Similar usage to "Babe" or "Sweetie". Variants include, dollywally, dollykins, dollywallykins, etc. From the Gimadran word *doulchika* meaning sweet little girl.

Dram – as a measurement of time, 50 drops or approximately a minute. Originates with the Freelands' use of waterclocks.

Drop – as a measurement of time, about a second. i.e. "Hold a drop!" meaning "Wait a second."

Mistress of the Golden Cords

Dref - schlock. Corny or overused subject matter as from a song or play. From the

Gimadran word, *drepha* meaning "happy" as used in *pryohka drepha*, a slapstick comedy play. rel. "dreffy"

Flob - To stand idly about with no particular purpose. i.e. to "flob about" means to "hang out."

Frepp - An awkward, useless person. From the Gimadran *phrepongo*, a criminal who keeps getting caught.

Freppish - Similar usage to "wussy", but with more of a furtive, nervous, and possibly guilty connotation.

Fuzzberries – Testicles. Also, an actual variety of berry covered with an inedible light purple, fuzzy rind. The taste is like a lychee berry crossed with a kiwifruit.

Gonnyrot – The infamous sexually transmitted pox that plagued the early Mystican settlers of the Freelands. The name "Gonny" is a derisive term for Yllgoni people, particularly the sailors from Yllgon who were thought to be the origin of the virus.

Guvny – Prudish. From the word governor, the highest state office in the Freelands.

Harkey – a.k.a. Harkey Coach. Preferred means of public transportation in Angelwood and many other Freelandish poleis. Horse drawn carriages with wide seats named for the Harceigh Region of Corwbha which supplied early Freelandish settlers with horses.

Hedwig – i.e. "going hedwig". Angry to the point of insanity. Refers to a famous Angelwood councilman named Hedwig who was known to fly into fits of rage (see chucking buckets).

Honi – Vagina; same usage as "pussy". Pronounced HOH-nee. From the Gimadran *Chahoni* or feminine principle. Commonly punned with the Mystican common word "honey" in colloquialisms, i.e. "He put his dipper in her honeypot."

Jawdy - sleazy. From the Gimadra *Mahkjohdhi* meaning the same.

Kapistarosolam – "Land of mindless indulgence". Derisive Syndraxan colloquialism for the Empire of Gimadra

Koudga – Unfortunate fellow or chap (usually, but not always, male). From the Gimadran *tikaojana* meaning "a slave who shovels manure".

Koke – Same usage as "cool". From the Gimadran *Kahokeh* meaning "rod of authority" - their divine masculine principal.

Kokachoni - Copacetic, having pleasant, mellow vibes. From the Gimadran *Kahokeh i'Chahoni* - their divine balance of masculine and feminine energies. *Chahoni* means "cavern of spirits".

Kull – Same usage as "ass", usually in reference to the anatomical part, not the type of person.

Kullbung – Same usage as "asshole", more commonly in reference to the type of person, rather than the anatomical part.

Mog – Head. Possibly of ancient Medanite origins; same root meaning of the name "Mogu", who is the god of performers, thieves, and basically anyone who has to think on his/her feet.

Mog-blotted – muddle-headed, as from regular consumption of alcohol.

Muddlemog – a ditzy, careless person. One who obsesses over useless things.

Mistress of the Golden Cords

Noddies – testicles. From the Mystican Common word nodule meaning small knot or knob.

Palabhandi – "Backwards land": the derisive Gimadran colloquialism for the Syndraxan Empire.

Palacka – adj. stupid; mentally deficient, or n. one who is lacking in basic mental functions. From the Gimadran *palah gahti* meaning backward-moving.

Palagong – slow, apathetic, backwards thinking or moving.

Pish – To ruin, dismiss, or make valueless. From the Gimadran *pishwa* meaning rubbish.

Pish ya pisser – To destroy one's credibility or reputation.

Pock – To use sexually. Also used as a generic vulgarity, i.e. "Get that pocking carriage out of the way!" or "The staveman caught me stealing, so now I'm pocked!" Originated with the rampant sexually transmitted diseases when the Freelands were first being colonized.

Pockstocker - a whoremonger or pimp.

Pongo – A Gimadran term of endearment meaning "big, dumb, and lovable person". From the Gimadran word *phrepongo* meaning a criminal who always gets caught.

Poofy - An effeminate man. Unknown origin.

Prassy – Behaving with the fussiness of a spoiled princess. Unknown origin.

Rach - Pronounced "rawch". To beat. From the Gimedran *warachee*, which is a type of sandal often used by Gimadran peasant women to beat unruly children.

Rock-mogged – Stupid. Having a head like a rock.

Adam Berk

Shest – Vulgar term for fecal excrement i.e. "trollshest".

Shest Bucket – A chamber pot.

Shestmog – One with disgusting values. One who has a head full of shest.

Shest Shover – Offensive term for a gay man.

Snarf – To caress with tongue and mouth.

Sneck – A kiss or to kiss.

Snollygoster – A clever, unscrupulous person.

Snollygeck - To kiss with tongue and groping. To take advantage of sexually.

Snollyhole – One's mouth, especially if one is a snollygoster.

Sparge – Ejaculate or the act of ejaculating

Specky – Amazing to behold. From the Mystican Common word *spectacular*.

Stalk – The male member, especially when erect, a.k.a. pockstalk

Stalkpocker - Someone (usually a man) who has promiscuous sex with (other) men.

Stalk-steered – The condition of being driven primarily by one's desire for sex. syn. wand-willed

Teedee – "Very". From the Gimadran, *atido*.

Twinklies – Eyes, especially those of a pretty girl (i.e. twinklie blues)

Vacky – Shallow. Having no intellectual depth.

Mistress of the Golden Cords

Vix – A beautiful woman whose beauty endows her with an inflated sense of entitlement. Same usage as "bitch" but with more positive connotation.

Wig off – To upset to the point of violence. Ref. Councilman Hedwig, see above.

ABOUT THE AUTHOR

In the early 2000s Adam Berk went to college in Los Angeles to study film, and stayed there to try to be a movie star. After growing disgusted with the entertainment industry (and his many unsuccessful attempts to be a part of it), he got a Master's of Professional Writing degree from the University of Southern California and left town. He now lives in Salem Massachusetts where he tends bar, studies the occult with his witchy wife, and writes silly stories about magic and mythic creatures. He has never been happier.

Made in United States
North Haven, CT
02 July 2022

20875052R00050